End Dream

End Dream

Angela Steed

Black Lyon Publishing, LLC

END DREAM
Copyright © 2012 by ANGELA STEED

Our books may be ordered through your local
bookstore or by visiting the publisher:

BlackLyonPublishing.com

Black Lyon Publishing, LLC
PO Box 567
Baker City, OR 97814

This is a work of fiction. All of the characters,
names, events, organizations and conversations
in this novel are either the products of the author's
vivid imagination or are used in a fictitious way for
the purposes of this story.

ISBN-10:   1-934912-44-1
ISBN-13:   978-1-934912-44-7

Written, published and printed in
the United States of America.

**Black Lyon
Publishing
Lyonettes
Paranormal
Romance**

To Kana:
*If the zombie apocalypse should arise, let's skip
the salads and find a greasy cheeseburger instead.
Sadly, I'd probably still get the salad—less meat for
the zombies to chew on. Thanks for being such a
dear friend. I'll miss you when you leave.*

Chapter One

Kira Spence puckered her rose-colored lips as she scanned the short line of shoes on the floor beside her bed. Her shoes were a pathetic display, dusty from lack of wear, all way older than she was. One pair was over forty years old, but was an interesting tall-heeled golden-strapped number dated back to the 1970s. Her older brother Jake had found the gaudy things in some abandoned warehouse in California five years prior, and for some reason thought she'd like them. Not that she didn't appreciate her estranged brother doing something nice for her, but at the time, she'd expressed her utter disappointment in his choice of gifts. Now they'd become somewhat of a shrine in her room, a memory she would never wear but could never dream of parting with.

It wasn't that there was a shortage of shoes in the world. She was sure there were plenty left. But shoes were rare on military bases like this one where nobody would dare venture outside. So the women around her took pride in showing off their rare collections of fancy footwear and dresses by clomping around the civilian section, inadvertently rubbing her nose in the fact she couldn't be feminine all day every day.

Being the only service woman stationed here, she didn't have any choice but to wear her standard-issue heavy black boots, navy blue cargo pants, and a light gray button-up shirt that fit too snug around her neck. Though fancy shoes and dresses were all material to her anyway, tonight was a special night, and she wished she had something nicer to wear.

She put on her only pair of blue jeans and her favorite dark blue tank top, the outfit she wore on those rare occasions she went out, which was fine with her. Wearing long pants covered the long unsightly scar on the calf of her right leg, the scar she had no recollection of getting. Jake told her it had something to do with the car accident she was in the day the virus made its way into the world—the time when hundreds of people died and yet came back as something else—monsters with an appetite for flesh. Jake also told her she was lucky she couldn't remember anything prior to six years ago, before the accident, and had left it at that.

Deciding on wearing her favorite flat black sandals she loved to shuffle around her room in, she slipped them on her bare feet. She wiggled her petite toes then inspected the small white tear on one of the leather bound straps draped over the top of her right foot. She cringed at the mere thought of them falling apart before the night was over, but these would have to do.

Kira gazed at her pale reflection in the narrow

full-length mirror on the wall. Her bangs had no curl as they hung straight down catching in her eyelashes. She brushed the strands to the side so she could inspect the long thin brown curls that strung past her shoulders.

Short hair was normally required in the military. But as assistant to Claven Calhoun, commander of the entire Oklahoma City base, she got away with tying her hair back instead. Since she was also the only female under his command, she knew he went easy on her, allowing her to get away with more than her fair share of broken regulations. This night though, she'd decided to let her hair down and not worry about what anyone else thought.

Not that it was particularly special that her long time friend Sam Riles, special operative and one of the few heroes of the somber world, was visiting this week. This time, whether he knew it or not, he'd flown in on her birthday. Sam only came in every six months to visit his younger brother Pete, but always set aside time for her. He was protective, caring ... friendly, which were all the traits Jake never had. Jake always blamed his lack of compassion on his important, top-secret position in the military. But Sam? He was Jake's right hand man, taking on the same pressures, if not more, and yet Sam managed to make a point to be here for her when she needed him.

Kira turned off the light then hurried out the door and into the hall, eager to get to Sam before he was smothered in officers and civilians wanting to hear about his latest adventures. She knew it was probably too late for that since it was already six in the evening, and thankfully still light outside.

The setting sun felt good on her bare arms as she made her way to the security gate where heavily armed guards stood waiting. She lifted her I.D. badge from her jean pocket and presented it to the guard who halted her.

"Going to The Den tonight, Kira?" he asked as he took the badge from her grasp. He inspected it briefly then handed it back to her.

"Yeah, Frances," she replied with a smile. It was comical that he was still required to see her identification after all these years.

"I hear Sam's over there now," Frances continued with a nod. "One of the guys who came through said he's got a pretty crazy story this time. I'm heading over there after my shift. Maybe I'll see you there." He shifted his weight to his right leg then cleared his throat. "The ladies will be there as usual, right?"

It was true. The women on the base adored Sam, though he never seemed to take notice at all the batting eyes. He kept his attention on everyone who crowded around him waiting to hear him speak. Kira enjoyed listening to his new stories, though she thought most were tragic. As a soldier Sam had seen a lot of action in his lifetime, a lot of death and decay during the alleged biochemical attack six years before. She knew Sam had to be traumatized to some degree, though he never outwardly showed it, always flashing that handsome grin of his, happily giving these people what they wanted to hear.

The first thing Kira saw when she walked through

the front doors of The Den was commander Claven. He stood at the end of the bar with a shot of vodka in hand drowning out the day's events.

Kira gave a sly grin as she went straight to him and saluted. "Commander."

"You've lost your mind, Spence," Claven muttered under his breath. She could see the playful smirk on the corner of his wrinkled mouth showing he'd been here for a while. "We're off duty and you're at the wrong table."

"Sorry, sir," she replied as she scoured the room with her eyes. "Force of habit to address my superior."

"You need to get out of your room more, young lady. Toss a few drinks back and relax for awhile. You're dismissed."

Kira bumped his arm playfully then wandered toward the large group in the back of the room. They were quiet, entranced, focusing their attention on the center of their circle. Though she couldn't see Sam at all, she heard the familiar soothing tenor of his that sent her skin tingling.

She squeezed in between two rather large men, both officers who were stationed near the back tower of the base. They glanced down at her briefly then smiled in greeting as she stepped a little farther toward the heart of the group.

"We'd found an entire colony of survivors - one hundred people," she heard Sam say. She still couldn't see him, but could tell she was getting closer by the volume of his voice. "We quarantined them at first then sent in CDC to make sure they weren't infected."

"Were they?" a soft female voice asked from the

group somewhere behind him.

"Not one," he replied. "They'd been living in the cave of the mountain, sending out scouts every day to find supplies and possibly more survivors. The nearby field was a prospering garden."

"They were outside ... gardening?" the soft voice interrupted, a little louder than before.

The entire group seemed to lean to Sam in unison. Kira waited to hear his answer as she pushed through the small crowd.

"Yeah," he said. "They were outside seemingly unafraid." He gave a short laugh through his nose. "There were also ... children, about twenty of them playing with each other as their parents worked in the field."

"Children?" another young woman said amongst whispers and gasps from the others around her. As Kira moved in beside her, she saw tears in the woman's eyes, a clear sign of hope, of what could be. Sam's stories were usually frightening, but obviously weren't always about the monsters roaming the earth.

When Sam finally came into sight, Kira's heart sank. He sat in the booth on the other side of his brother Pete, small glass of vodka in hand and elbows pointed outward on the wooden table in front of him. His short sandy blond hair looked like silk beneath the low light of the white hanging lamp. Those perfectly sculpted muscles flexed under his tight navy blue shirt as he stood up from the table to greet her.

He flashed that perfect smile when he scooped her up in his strong arms. "Kira!" he said as he whirled her around once then set her back down on her feet. "Wow," he continued, not letting her get a word in, "look at the rose in your cheeks. You've been eating better."

She couldn't help but laugh. The last time he'd visited he'd told her she looked pale and needed to eat more. She hadn't the heart to tell him her diet was the same, that he was only embarrassing her in front of all these people. Thankfully they were beginning to move toward the bar to refresh their empty glasses.

Pete scooted over giving Kira room to sit down, but Sam pulled her over to his side of the table instead. He threw his arm around her shoulders then squeezed her tightly several times.

"So you rescued all those people," she said as Sandy, the waitress, set a glass of vodka on the table.

"Yeah, while investigating a disturbance on the outer edge of Kansas City. Jayson heard their distress signal. I think the people had forgotten about the recording over the years."

Kira gazed up into his light blue eyes. He seemed different. The usual short wrinkles on the outer corners of his eyes wrinkled just a little more when he smiled. He was only thirty-four, still young and impeccably strong. Right now he looked older, exhausted.

"What did you do with them?" she asked turning her attention on her drink, indulging in a sip.

"We left them there," he replied.

"You left them alone?"

"We assigned several guards to help them out. They have a good thing going," he added then cleared his throat as if maybe he had doubts about it. "It's better than this, Kira. People here are sheltered but unfortunately your supplies are running low."

Kira suddenly caught his hand and pulled it beneath the table. It wasn't unusual for him to hold her hand, especially when he told her negative things like that. She knew supplies were limited, and they'd eventually need to start sending soldiers out for supplies, but she just didn't want to hear.

"I'm sorry." He gently squeezed her hand. "Let's just drink and enjoy tonight. After all, we do have a birthday to celebrate."

The corners of Kira's mouth rose. He'd remembered. Even Claven hadn't wished her a happy birthday today. Not that she minded. She'd rather forget the embarrassing song and stick with something quiet like this moment with Sam.

"So how old are you now?" Pete asked with a humored grunt. "Forty?"

"Ah man, Pete," Sam remarked. "You're not supposed to ask a lady her age."

Kira took a big gulp of her drink. Her eyes watered a little as the fluid burned down her throat. It'd been months since she'd had an alcoholic beverage, actually during the last time Sam had visited the base. It wasn't going to take much to start feeling the effects.

"It's okay, Sam," she said, giving Pete's shin a quick kick under the table. "I'm twenty-nine today." Unfortunately her voice carried to the table behind her where two men burst out in song. And it only took one verse of the dreaded birthday song for the entire bar to join in on her humiliation.

Kira let go of Sam's hand so she could hide her face. She peeked through her fingers to find Sandy carrying a large rectangular birthday cake with two lit candles on top. Sandy set it down in front of her then leaned back with a guilty smirk on her wrinkled face.

"I'm sorry," Sandy said as she pushed her short gray curls behind her ears. "Claven and I were going to make you a real cake, but you know that'd require flour. I made this out of rice and sweetened it up a bit with fruit. I imagine it tastes a little like a custard."

"Oh, thanks," Kira grumbled shyly, feeling warmth in her face when she blew out the fire on the candles. Not that she didn't like the attention, but being the only female soldier on the base, God knew she got enough of it already. It was nice that everyone had remembered her birthday, but she'd rather have spent it quietly in her room like she'd done in the past.

"I brought you something," Sam said. "I couldn't help thinking of you when I saw them."

As long as Kira had known him, he'd never brought her any real presents, at least none that were wrapped. He'd always been a very strong man with superior control over his emotions. And though he was always quite caring when it came to her, this kind display with everyone else watching was so unlike him.

Sandy picked up the cake and placed it on the table behind her giving Sam room to set the plain white box with the glittering purple tie down in front of Kira. Kira stared at it in awe then glanced around her, catching the eyes of every person in the room. Even Claven gave her a quick wink, his smirk still lingering on his old tired face.

Kira cleared her throat nervously then carefully untied the box. She lifted the lid and pulled back a soft white cloth to reveal the most precious thing she'd ever seen. It was a gift from the outside world—a pair of black dress sandals similar to the ones she wore now. But these were new and clean and more importantly—from Sam.

Tears welled in her eyes. She heard the other women in the room gasp then whisper amongst themselves the exact thoughts rolling through her mind. Sam was the most amazing man in the world.

"Oh, Sam," she whispered. She raised the sandals from the box as if they were made of glass. The tag was still on them, making this gift that much more special.

"I know, I know," he replied shyly when she kissed his smooth warm cheek. "Now let's celebrate."

Chapter Two

The room spun. It wasn't so bad that Kira couldn't stand on her own, but she definitely needed a little help from Sam. Even though he was almost as wobbly as she was, he was still an excellent crutch.

Kira had never seen The Den more hopping than it was tonight. Drinks were on Sam, always on him when he flew in a few cases of liquor. He also brought in as many rations as he could fit in the crate beneath his helicopter, though each trip there were a little less than before.

Kira listened as he told his story to Frances who'd come as soon as his shift at the gate was over. Although there'd been request after request for Sam to tell the same story, he didn't mind telling it again and she didn't mind listening to him. His voice was soothing and perfect. She believed he could be a spokesman for the military, easing the minds of the weary, giving pep talks when the soldiers' spirits were low. He also had the looks, the comforting, easy-on-the-eyes kind. It was obvious every single woman wanted to be near him. Some had even touched his hand, hoping he'd notice. He'd oblige with a kind word or two, but then settle back in his place next to her.

Kira couldn't stop staring at him, watching him smile as those big blue eyes gazed at whomever he spoke to. His long dark lashes were perfectly spaced and curled exquisitely upward. To be thinking about devilishly handsome Sam like this, wanting him to notice her just as much as the other women here was something she'd never wanted before. The only difference was, tonight he seemed to notice her, too.

She laughed under her breath. He was her closest friend, the protective brother she never had. She didn't want that tonight. What had changed? Was it the way he looked at her, the way he touched her as if she were a delicate flower? She shivered, excited to think what had changed were their feelings for each other.

She'd had a crush on him when she met him six years ago some time after the accident. The attraction was an immediate thing, but she'd never told him purely out of respect. Sam was her superior. Though military ranks really didn't count anymore when it came to relationships, she'd used that as an excuse to get over her crush and think of him as a friend.

Kira switched her stance, taking her weight off Sam's arm. How silly she was for allowing her crush to come back now when, to him, she would always be Jake's little sister. Jake was his superior, and messing with his little sister would probably get Sam into a world of trouble. Not that she could ever see Jake really giving a damn about what she did, since they'd barely spoken a word to each other since the shoes incident. Jake would more likely tell her to back off of his crew.

Kira could barely hold her head up any longer, not so much from being drunk from the many glasses of vodka she'd downed, but from being tired as well. It had been a long day.

She caught Sam's attention by leaning her face against his biceps. *Oh my*, she thought when he put his arm around her shoulders. He smelled unbelievably good, like sweet musk and a hint of wooden spice.

She laughed drunkenly when he turned his gaze on her. "I think ... I need to go to my room," she said hearing the slur in her words. She ducked under his arm, moving away from his warm touch before she got too caught up in him to leave. "We're still on for dinner tomorrow night, right? Carrots and steamed rice," she added as he walked with her toward the booth.

"I wouldn't miss it," he replied catching her arm before she stumbled into the table. "Whoa now. I'm not sure you're sober enough to walk home on your own."

She gathered her beautiful new shoes in her arms then turned to Pete. He sat with a frown, his arm around a very pretty young woman with head of golden blond hair. It was Jill, his on-again, off-again girlfriend. She didn't look thrilled, as usual, that Pete looked concerned over Kira's well-being.

"You're both smashed." Pete retracted his arm from Jill's shoulders. "Let me walk Kira home," he said as he began to slide out of the booth.

"Oh, come on. I'm fine. Stay here and have a good time." Kira smiled at Jill who nodded in agreement as she twirled her finger around one of those beautiful curls resting on her neckline.

"It's okay, Pete," Sam chimed in, stopping his brother from rising to his feet. "I won't let Kira get caught in a cluster of zombies." Kira tossed him a scowl. He knew how much she hated it when he talked about the dead wandering around outside, and yet he still loved to tease her. "Don't worry. I'll get you to your door safely."

Pete didn't look thrilled. In the years Kira had known him, he'd become somewhat of a protective brother too. They definitely bickered like siblings, but he'd always been there for her when she needed him. With Sam here now, he could relax and have a little fun for a change. He didn't need to worry, though she could see it all over his sulking face.

"I'll be fine," she emphasized. She closed her eyes for a moment then opened them when Sam grasped her hand.

He pulled her out the exit door then stopped at the top of the outside steps. "Great," he remarked as he gazed out over the dimly lit walkway leading toward the security gate. He let go of her hand then zipped up his dark blue jacket.

It was pouring rain. Kira could barely walk in her torn sandals now, so running across the wet ground in these old things, especially drunk, was going to be tricky.

"We could wait until the storm's over," she offered

as she clutched her new shoes tightly in her arms. She definitely didn't want these to ruin.

He pulled her shoes from her arms with his left hand then reached for her with his right. "A little rain won't hurt us," he said, grasping her hand firmly.

He pulled her out with him in the rain. They ran down the walkway at a pace she could keep up with her old shoes barely hanging on. The rain was relentless, torture on her almost bare feet, cold on her skin. She shivered, squeezing her toes for traction every time she stepped.

This part of the walk usually scared her at night, knowing there were monsters just over the twenty foot wall to her right. On her left were old empty storage units with dark crevices between the walls, a perfect hiding place for some civilian hoodlum awaiting his unsuspecting victim. But she was with Sam now, and he'd never let anything happen to her. Sam knew how to handle anything, especially when it came to dangerous situations, including dealing with the undead.

Suddenly finding this run through the rain exhilarating, Kira pulled her hand away from his and stopped. She couldn't remember the last time she'd done anything like this, and wanted to bask in the moment.

The security gate was ahead, lit with spotlights glowing in the rain. Only thirty more yards and she'd be under the roof of the barracks. She'd be dry, ready to pass out on her bed and sleep off this drunken crush. But for some reason, she didn't want to leave this spot. She wanted to be here in the rain, hidden in the dark with Sam.

"What are you doing, Kira?" Sam asked trying to nudge her gently down the path.

She twirled around and laughed, happily drunk … just plain happy. "It's my birthday, Sam," she replied, stopping her dance to look upward into the dark sky. The cold droplets felt wonderful on her warm face. "I should be able to do this at least once a year without someone telling me it's silly." She stuck out her tongue to taste the water. Maybe it was completely childish, and maybe she was making a fool out of herself in front of him. But right now it didn't matter. It was the first time in months that she'd felt safe enough to enjoy a moment outside.

Sam's hands were suddenly on her shoulders pushing her toward the black opening between two storage buildings. He held tightly so she wouldn't stumble and fall in the dark, or turn around and run straight back out into the rain. Being under the overhang was not as much fun as dancing in the downpour.

Kira turned around to scold him for ruining her moment but held her tongue. There was enough light from the opening to see that impressive, comforting smile of his. His face was close enough for her to see those brilliant blue eyes gazing down at her.

"Happy birthday," he whispered then shrugged as he stood upright. He stuffed his hands in the front pockets of his jacket then looked toward the walkway as if meaning to leave. "We should get you to your room before you catch a chill."

Kira leaned back against the storage building's

wall. Her heart pounded as thoughts of being with him skittered through her mind. He'd come so close to her, closer than he'd ever been before. Maybe it was the alcohol in her bloodstream, but she couldn't shake the feeling he wanted to be with her too.

"Sam," she said as she grabbed two fistfuls of his jacket. She pulled him to her then quickly pressed her lips to his. It was a sweet kiss, no tongue, definitely something neither of them had ever shared. He'd always kissed her temple or the top of her head, usually in greeting or departing, and she'd always kissed his cheek. This was the first time their mouths actually pressed together.

When she parted from him she breathed deeply. She snickered when she saw his widened eyes. Shock was definitely in those beautiful blues.

"I've been wanting to do that for a very long time," she confessed, pulling him close again. "Besides the shoes, I couldn't have asked for a better birthday gift. Except for maybe ..."

"Stop Kira," he warned. He swallowed hard as he pried her hands loose from his jacket then forced them down to her sides. "I can't do this with you."

"It's okay," she whispered, sliding her hand down his strong arm, feeling it tense up with her touch. She grasped his hand in hers then gently squeezed as she gazed at him. "I understand why you don't want to be with me." He opened his mouth to speak but she pressed her finger to his lips, shushing him. "I know all the excuses you want to make. I'm too drunk or I'm Jake's little sister. But as inebriated as I am right now, I know exactly what I want. That's you, Sam. I want to be with you here ... now."

She pulled his hand around her waist then played with the top button of his jeans until it came undone. When she tugged on his zipper he quickly caught her hand.

"Kira," he said, brows lowered against his eyes, smile suddenly replaced with a scowl.

She pulled her hand away from his then quickly pressed her palm against the front of his jeans. A wicked grin crept over her face. He was hard. That meant she was getting to him. He wanted her just as much as she wanted him.

"Just go with it, Sam," she whispered, sliding her hand along his bulge, slowly working her hand inside his jeans until she grasped hold of his erection. "Let this happen."

He leaned back and gazed at her for a long moment. He closed his eyes then let out a short breath as she gently stroked the length of him, pulling him from the confines of his pants.

"Kira, please." He groaned, placing his palms against the wall on each side of her head. "Don't do this."

For a moment she feared he'd gain his composure, shove her hand away and tell her she was a stupid girl. In fact, she half expected him to move back and leave her there alone without saying another word. But he surprised her.

His mouth was suddenly over hers, tongue against her tongue. His hands frantically grasped the top of her pants then shoved them down over her hips to her ankles. Then they were off, torn shoes caught inside and crumpled on the ground next to her bare feet.

He lifted her up against him then pulled her legs around his waist. As he walked with her through the dark alley, she threw her arms around his neck and hung on. Her head swam from the liquor but more so from the ache of the moment. This was what she wanted, what she'd longed for all night. The surreal moment of being with Sam Riles was going to happen.

She lost her breath when her back touched the cold surface of the brick wall, then again when he entered her. She hadn't expected it to happen so suddenly and never dreamed he'd be so rough. He penetrated her so hard and fast it caused pain, almost bringing her to tears. With his mouth against hers, she couldn't catch her breath. She shoved at his chest and whined until finally he stopped.

He leaned his head back to look at her. "What's wrong?"

"Please slow down," she whimpered.

He grasped her face in his hands. "I'm sorry." He kissed her gently this time, passionately as he slowed to deep, sensual movements.

"This shouldn't be happening," she heard him whisper as if he'd said it into her ear though his warm lips moved against the bridge of her cheek. Her skin rose with a chill as he ran his tongue down her neck and his hands up inside her shirt and bra. Cool fingers found her nipples and massaged gently, setting her insides on fire.

"She's so beautiful," his whisper came again, a little louder in her ear. "I can't help myself," he groaned as he thrust a little harder. By his chanting breath, he was on the brink of release. With his skin against hers, and the smooth motion of his hips, she couldn't hold out any longer.

His breath was muffled as he buried his face on her chest. She felt the jolt of his erection and then his warmth flood inside her. She closed her eyes, enjoying the moment, not wanting it to end as she too came for him. Breath erratic, she held him tightly around the neck until the ache inside her calmed.

"Oh Sam," she breathed in delight. "That was … amazing."

She wanted to hear him return with his own fulfilled words, but he didn't say a word. His breath came faster as his body began to tremble. Heat emanated off his skin quickly building up intensity until Kira's moment of ecstasy turned to excruciating pain.

Her skin suddenly burned as if she'd slid into a tub of scalding water. She cried out as her insides felt like it was on fire. But it only lasted for second as Sam quickly let her down from the wall and pulled away.

Kira fell to the ground on her backside watching in horror as blue flames danced over his entire body. The azure light rolled for a moment longer then quickly faded into shadow. The scent of Sam's musk permeated the air as if she'd just sprayed his cologne all around her.

"Sam!" she cried out when he fell to his knees. She reached for him.

"Stay back," he growled, stopping her from getting too close.

Kira stared in utter dismay, wondering what in the world had just happened. Shaken by this sudden change in him, she gathered her pants near her feet. She hurriedly stepped into them then slid them up around her waist.

"Sam … " she said in a strangled voice as he stood on his feet. "What was that?"

He drew in a deep breath then reached for her. She stepped back once, but he reached further, catching her face in his hands before she could get away.

"I'm so sorry," he pleaded, leaning his temple against hers, massaging her face as he wiped her tears with his thumbs. "I've never lost control like that before."

"Control?" she asked in a panic. She moaned, feeling rather dizzy and a little sick. Her legs grew weak, but he caught her in his arms before she slumped over to the ground.

The alcohol had finally taken its toll. The tension release with Sam, then the intense burning of her body, must have sent her into such an exhausted state that she just couldn't recover from it tonight. Sleep was inevitable.

"I've failed you, Kira," she heard him whisper as he picked her up in his arms. "I promised that I'd always keep you safe, but I have failed."

Chapter Three

Kira knew her birthday was over when Claven made a point to yell at her. She'd come in ten minutes after seven, and that was ten minutes too late. He'd resorted to name-calling, telling her she was a subordinate assistant, his usual name for her when she did something wrong or was late for duty. She'd pulled a short fake grin from somewhere inside her, but he'd called her out on it yelling that she should never smile again unless it was real. Hence the frown she wore now would linger for the rest of the day.

There was a reason for her frown. She hadn't seen Sam since she'd passed out the night before in her room. If he'd followed his routine he would've stopped by at her work a few times already. Once to remind her of the dinner she was cooking for him that night, and once to escort her to his helicopter where she would add the supplies he'd brought to the inventory sheet.

Inventory was an important part of her job. Claven, God help the man, had yelled at her again for not getting it finished before noon. Now she had to work through lunch to find Sam, then get him to sound off the supplies while she wrote them down.

She entered the hangar, arms wrapped tightly around her large black notebook, nervous. She clutched her pen in her right hand as she moved toward the shiny black helicopter sitting in the center of the warehouse. Sam stood on the other side of it with Pete inspecting what looked to be a loose metal panel on the floor of the craft. Pete glanced at her, followed by Sam. They looked at each other briefly then went back to removing the misfit piece.

Great, Kira thought to herself. Pete probably knew what happened between her and Sam last night, and most likely every single detail. He wasn't the kind to joke about something like this, but he was probably going to be pissed at her for her momentary lack of judgment. Her excuse, and the only thing she could think of, was that she was utterly drunk.

"Hungover?" Pete said with a chuckle.

She stopped on the other side of the small open-door helicopter and set her notebook down on the floor of it. "Not much," she said in a soft voice though her head had hurt a little earlier this morning.

"I heard Claven's been yelling at you all day," Pete continued.

She shrugged. "You know the Commander, always taking things out on the ones he loves."

Pete laughed heartily. Things must have gone well with Jill last night. Kira would love to tell him everything went well for her too, but Sam had avoided her all morning. And, besides the one glance, he hadn't even acknowledged she was here.

"Claven's angry about the inventory at the moment," she said directing her words at Sam, who had moved his attention to attaching the new floor panel. "He wants me to get this done before the day's end so we can start distributing supplies to the proper channels."

"Yeah," Sam finally said in a rather cold tone. "Give me a minute to finish these repairs then we'll start."

Kira picked up her notebook. Sam still didn't look at her, neither did he crack his usual sweet grin. If only Pete would leave so she could talk to him, to apologize profusely for throwing herself at him. Then she would find out how he almost burned her alive with some unworldly glow, though that part was still a little fuzzy. She wasn't even sure it had happened at all, convincing herself that it'd all been a terrible dream.

"So Claven's got you working through lunch, huh?" Pete said checking his watch. "It's twelve now," he added, his voice echoing through the hangar.

Kira shrugged as she sat down on the edge of the chopper. "I missed breakfast this morning too. I guess I'll be starving when dinner comes around." Sam finally flashed her another quick glance.

Pete shoved his hands in his pockets then harrumphed. "The cooks are serving chicken in the cafeteria today. First time in a year and I'm not going to miss the opportunity," he remarked as he ambled around the front of the helicopter and headed toward the exit. "I'll bring you guys some if there's any left."

Kira watched Pete stroll across the hangar, his

footsteps echoing until he disappeared out the tall open door. She was surprised he didn't give her any cynical sass about throwing herself at his brother, but then maybe he didn't know what happened between them.

Deciding it didn't really matter, she turned her attention on Sam who had just finished his repairs. He ran his hand across the floor checking for uneven corners. Finding a smooth finish, he picked up the screwdriver Pete had left on the floor then headed toward the back room where the tools were kept.

Kira watched him walk away. She desperately wanted to say something to make him stop and pay attention to her, but her throat felt tight until he disappeared through the tool room door.

She leaned her head back against the pilot's seat then closed her eyes. This was agony. Sam was torturing her with the silent treatment. Not that she blamed him, but at least he could say something, anything to make her feel a little taller than an inch.

"The crate's over here," Sam called out, startling her into opening her eyes. Her heart practically leapt from her chest. "Let's just get this over with so I can get back to work."

Kira hopped off the edge of the chopper and ambled his way, watching him as he pried open the large wooden crate. His strong arms tensed as he wedged the flat end of the crowbar in between the front and top crevice of the box. He pulled until the door cracked open and fell with a deafening bang at her feet.

He tossed the crowbar to the floor, causing

another ear-piercing echo throughout the hangar and in Kira's sensitive ears. Then Sam ducked into the crate to begin retrieving supplies.

"There's the usual three, fifty-pound bags of rice in here," he said as she came to stand at the entrance. He lifted all three large brown sacks and pushed past her to the empty wooden pallet along the hangar's wall.

She opened the notebook and skimmed the list of supplies until she found the entry for rice. The base only had three bags left. Though they were expecting another large shipment in a month or so, six bags of rice would last at least three.

He shoved past her again and into the crate. He still wouldn't look at her, treating her as if she were some unrecognized private in the military. She thought maybe he just wanted to get the job done fast so they could talk without interruption, but then he'd never given her a silent treatment before.

"Sam," she said as he picked up a crate of ripe apples. She reached out and touched his forearm, but he ignored her, quickly heading out to the pallet where he'd set down the rice. When he set the crate down, he heaved a sigh.

She turned her attention to the notebook then put a mark in the empty slot beside apples. This hurt more than she'd wanted it to. She'd prepared herself for a lecture or possibly an excuse that they were both drunk and it'd never happen again. But for him to be silent like this, ignoring her like she wasn't even here, made her insides churn. Tears crept into her eyes, just enough to make the words on the page in the notebook blurry.

Sam entered the crate again, but this time he met her gaze briefly as he passed. Then he stopped, hands gripping his sides as he turned around to face her.

"Damn," he said quietly as he stared at her. "Last night shouldn't have happened. You know that don't you?"

"I know," Kira responded with a sniffle. "It's my fault. I pushed myself on you."

"We were both drunk," he said. "We were caught up in the moment."

"Right … we," she said cynically.

He switched his weight to the other foot. "Yes, Kira … we. Don't think that I don't care about you because I do. But you and I … we can never be anything more. Do you understand?"

"Sure," she said softly, though her heart suddenly felt like it'd been dragged across the jagged earth and left out for the buzzards to pick apart. "Will you just answer one thing for me?"

"What is it?"

"That light," she said hoping she wasn't going to sound like a crazy person since she wasn't sure the light was even real. "Where did that light come from? What was it?"

"Something you shouldn't be asking about," he replied.

She breathed in relief. At least now she knew she hadn't dreamt it, but then the truth was staring at her in the face looking rather miffed that she was digging for the answer she already knew.

"I am asking. Are you … ?"

When he looked away she leaned on her heels suddenly finding her answer. She'd heard rumors through the ranks about a group of super soldiers who scouted the world ridding the planet of the infected. They were the military's biggest secret beginning way before doomsday began six years ago.

Never did she think Sam would be one of them, though now it made perfect sense. He was one of the strongest men she'd ever known, aside from her brother. And with the light she'd seen rolling from his body, there was no other explanation.

He shook his head, then gazed at her with those striking blue eyes. He moved closer to her. At first she thought maybe he would go back on his word and kiss her. She'd hoped. But instead he stopped within an inch of her face.

"You don't get it, Kira," he whispered, speaking not to her but at her as if he were her superior. He was her superior, but he'd never gotten in her face like she was some insignificant soldier with an attitude problem. "I could've killed you last night. If I hadn't pulled away when I did you'd be dead right now."

"But I'm not dead," she whispered, unable to back away, wanting to feel his arms around her again.

"I'm supposed to protect you, not put you in danger."

She opened her mouth to retort, but grew quiet when a group of men entered the hangar. They laughed and talked amongst themselves, voices echoing through the hangar as they headed their way. Claven had sent help with unloading.

"Are you still coming for dinner tonight?" she

whispered. "Please come. We need to talk more about this."

Sam shrugged then turned his attention to the bags behind him just in time for the four men to duck inside the crate. Though they were all slouching, they saluted Sam respectfully as they would their commander.

"At ease guys," Sam said, half-grin playing on his lips. "Let's just get these supplies to food storage before they rot."

•

Sam had brought in more supplies than she'd thought. It actually added up to be a few more of everything than the last bunch he'd brought in, which was a good thing. With the food storage stocked and inventory finally finished, Kira was ready to call it a day. And by the time Claven finally let her off duty, it was half past six.

She wasn't sure Sam would show up for dinner, but she went ahead and showered then put on the only dress she owned, which wasn't really a dress. The garment was anything but fancy, a simple black short sleeve top that hung down to her knees. She wrapped a thin dark blue belt around her waist then tied it in a bow in back. The neckline was shaped like a V letting her show a little of her feminine side, which was something she rarely did. But she figured since she had amends to make with Sam, she might as well dress up for the occasion.

She finished cooking dinner by seven and sat down at her tiny table next to her twin bed. She stared at the two empty plates for half an hour debating on whether she should go ahead and eat. Sam was only thirty minutes late, though he'd never kept her waiting more than five. It had been an exceptionally busy day for everyone so he was probably tired, crashed out on Pete's cot for the night, though that was highly unlikely.

Kira sighed heavily as she stuck her elbows on the table and leaned her chin on her fists. He wasn't coming. She'd really messed things up, so much he'd probably never speak to her again.

Maybe he had a good reason. Before this mess happened, she would've scolded him for being late. But since their beautiful friendship was on the rocks, she'd hold her tongue and accept his excuse no matter what it was.

A light knock came to the door. She hurriedly opened it to that same cold face he'd presented that afternoon.

"Kira," he said as she stepped aside letting him in. "I probably shouldn't have come."

"Why would you say that?" She shut the door knowing darn well why he didn't want to come.

Sam glanced at the set table. The bitterness in his gaze softened as he eyed the cooking pot that was still full. "You still haven't had anything to eat today?"

She shook her head as she sat down at the table. "I've been waiting for you."

Sam picked up both plates and set them on the short narrow counter of the kitchen. He lifted the glass lid on the pot then breathed in deep. "It smells good," he said, spooning out a small portion onto both plates. He replaced the lid then set the plates back down on the table.

"Come on, Sam," she said as he stuffed a forkful of rice and carrots in his mouth. "I know you're still angry with me. Just let me have it. Give me a what for so you'll feel better."

He set his fork down on the plate then gave a distraught sigh. She was ever so glad to see his face soften and the right side of his mouth curve upward into a half-grin.

"Okay, Kira." He narrowed his eyes at her. "I regret what we did last night. It's all your fault for being out of your mind drunk and it will never happen again."

She leaned back against her chair and folded her arms over her chest. His words were more or less what she'd wanted to hear, but it made her heart sting like crazy. If he wasn't sitting here before her staring at her with that smug smirk on his face, she'd have flung herself down on her bed and bawled her eyes out.

"Well," she managed to choke out. "At least you were man enough to come here tonight to tell me this."

"What did you want me to say?" he asked. "You wanted me to blame you for what happened, right?"

"Yeah," she hesitantly replied. "You should be angry with me."

He slammed his hand down on the table startling her into silence. Her eyes were suddenly damp with tears now believing what they had before would never be again. But then he slid his palm over her cheek brushing his thumb gently against her wet skin.

"Kira," he said softly. "I could've stopped it from happening if I'd truly wanted to. I'm sorry if I acted like a jerk today." He brushed a lock of her hair behind her ear then gently kissed her temple. "I just ... wasn't sure what to do about the plan I had for you."

"What do you mean?" she asked with a sniffle.

"I've been thinking about something for a while now," he said as he leaned his elbows on his knees. "I wanted to take you out."

She gazed at him intently. After all the silent treatment and tears shed, he'd actually come here to ask her out on a date? She didn't know whether to be flattered, excited, or mad.

"Claven would never let me have the day off," she said. "And what exactly would we do? There's nothing here but The Den."

"No," he said with a chuckle. "I meant out there, away from the base. There's something wonderful out there and I want to show it to you."

She stood, heart suddenly pounding. "Away from the base?" A cold chill swept over her skin as the nightmarish visions of the dead surrounded her, closed in on her until they were on top of her gnawing at her flesh, just like the nightmares she had. "No, no, no, You know I can't do that. Claven wouldn't let me go anyway."

"I've already run it past him," he replied. "He says you haven't taken a day for yourself since you came here six years ago. He's already approved your leave."

She scowled when he came to her side. She hugged her arms and stepped back finding herself pinned against the wall, shivering. How could he go behind her back like this? He knew how much she dreaded the thought of going outside the base let alone actually doing it. She wouldn't go, plain and simple.

"Kira, honey," he said gently grasping her arms just below her shoulders. "I want you to see for yourself that there are people out there living safely, able to walk outside and breathe the fresh air. It's an amazing thing."

"I can't," she said firmly, though seeing such an impossible thing struck her interest.

"I'll be with you every step of the way. I swear you'll be perfectly safe." He pulled her into his arms then gazed down at her. "Please, Kira, do this for me?"

Oh that beautiful grin of his, it was terribly dangerous, just as dangerous as those gorgeous blue eyes shining down. He certainly knew how to move her. And no matter how frightened she was about going outside, how could she say no to him?

"On one condition," she finally said, sticking to her guns and hoping he wouldn't see how weak he made her.

"Anything," he replied confidently, standing upright and proud, prepared to fulfill her request.

"I want to know everything ... about you, all the secrets you're keeping about who you really are."

She leaned back on her right heel waiting for his response. He folded his arms over his chest and stared at her for a long moment, and then gave a quick nod.

"I'll tell you as much as I can once we've reached

our destination. Meet me in the hangar at O-six-hundred."

He turned away, but she caught him by the wrist and pulled him back around. "Wait. Where are you going?"

At first he stood there looking uncertain, but then his face softened just a little more. He gave her small peck on the cheek then quickly left her room.

Kira slumped, disappointed yet scared out of her wits. It'd been so long since she'd even looked over the towering walls around her, or had even wanted to. She'd had nightmares about it, seeing hordes of the dead desperately trying to break down the walls of the base. She'd pushed thoughts like that out of her mind, convincing herself that that's all it was, just nightmares; that there was nothing out there but empty streets.

If it were anyone else, she'd have stamped her foot down and immediately said no way, and that would've been that. But this was Sam Riles, the man she trusted with her life, the man she cared about more than any other person in the world. And if it turned out he was indeed the super soldier she thought him to be, then she'd be completely safe. Yet, she couldn't shake the feeling that leaving was a very bad idea.

Chapter Four

O-six-hundred came early. Though Kira barely slept a wink all night, she felt somewhat refreshed. After a shower and a little fruit medley from the cafeteria, she was as ready as she'd ever be to go on this trip with Sam. That was the plus side, of course—being with him.

Sam had already moved his helicopter out of the hangar and was ready to depart. The black metallic paint of the vessel reflected light from the morning sun blinding her just a little. She could see him. His sandy blond hair stood out against his black T-shirt tucked into tan cargo pants. Kira got a kick out of his choice of wear since it was almost the same dress she'd chosen for the day, except she wore a navy blue T instead of black.

As she neared the chopper, two other bodies came out of the hangar door. She wondered what Pete and Jill were doing as they slung their bags through the open back door of the helicopter. Realizing they were coming, too, she was slightly disappointed this trip

Sam coordinated wasn't just to get her alone. But she understood this mission was to let others see what he'd seen, and that there was still hope in the world.

"Good morning," Sam said grinning when she finally made it to his side. "Are you ready to go?"

Though her body trembled, she nodded. Sam took her small bag from her shoulder then put it in the back with the rest of the bags that seemed a tad overstuffed. She'd packed light—a pair of blue jeans, her favorite tanktop, and thin black jacket.

She also packed her long white shirt for sleeping as well as her new sandals in case they stayed the night. But by the looks of the other bags, it almost seemed like they were going to be gone for weeks instead of two days.

Kira's legs wobbled a little as she climbed into the co-pilot's seat. Sam pulled the belt over her shoulders then strapped her in, pulling once to make sure it was secure.

"We'll be fine," he said palming her cheek. "I won't let anything happen to you, okay? Just … do me a big favor." When she nodded he continued, "When we lift off the ground, keep your eyes forward. Do not look down. That's an order from your superior."

Kira couldn't believe he'd said that. It'd take a lot of effort not to let curiosity take over knowing she'd look just to see why she shouldn't. She was a soldier, sort of, though more of a combatant of paper to keep the commander on track. But she was, nonetheless, trained for combat.

He gently pushed the headset over her head then turned on the microphone. He gave her a quick wink then leaned back to close the door.

Kira breathed in deeply, closing her eyes for just a moment until she heard the engine start. The propellers began to wind then whir loudly.

"Here we go," Sam said, his voice analog but clear in her ears through the headset. "Keep your eyes to the skies ladies," he reminded.

Kira had forgotten all about Pete and Jill. She glanced back to find them sitting closely together. Pete looked at ease, but Jill was obviously petrified. Her face was pale, lips slightly blue and quivering noticeably. She didn't look like a girl venturing out to see something wonderful, but looked as if she were heading into a nightmare.

Kira was just as scared, but at least she knew how to handle her fear of flying. When she caught Jill's widened gaze, she smiled hoping her false calm would help put her at ease.

"It'll be okay," Kira told her through the headset.

Pete took hold of Jill's hand as the helicopter began to ascend.

Kira immediately turned to the front and grasped the bar on the door with a shaky hand. Her stomach churned a little as they rose to the top of the tower where heavily armed guards stood watching.

Just a few more feet and they'd be over the wall and the barbed wire fencing. "Don't look down," she whispered to herself. God knew she tried not to, but her eyes immediately turned to the ground. "Oh my god!" she shrieked, quickly covering her mouth with her unsteady hand as she scanned the moving ground.

There were thousands of them wandering on the streets, crowding around the base as they shoved and fought to get close to the walls where others tried to climb. Diseased faces turned to the skies reaching for the helicopter with pale blue arms as if pleading for them not to go.

Tears streamed Kira's face. With her hand still over her mouth, she leaned back on the seat and concentrated on her breathing. All this time they'd been surrounded by monsters and she'd never known. She'd never wanted to know and that's why she'd never went to the overlook. She wished to God she'd never looked down, because now she didn't want to go back. And two days from now, because of Sam's insistence to make her come, she would have to.

"I gave you an order, Kira!" Sam shouted startling her.

She wiped her tears with rigid fingers then looked at him. "I'm okay," she lied. "I had to see it. Oh God," she added as she closed her eyes. "I had to see it."

She suddenly felt Sam's hand on hers. He grasped firmly, gathering her attention on him. "You're safe," he said in his commanding voice. "Do you understand me?"

"Yes," she replied, though she couldn't get the images out of her mind. How much longer would the base walls hold before they finally found their way in? All those civilians and soldiers, including her—they'd never survive an attack that big.

She'd rather die than become some monster starving for human flesh. A chill worked through her but Sam's voice brought her back from her nightmarish thoughts. He'd responded to a call on another line coming through the headset. She couldn't hear who it was, but could hear Sam's replies clearly.

"Yes," Sam said aloud. "The light's left the base." He paused for a moment then responded again. "Roger that. ETA, three hours."

Kira closed her eyes and concentrated on calming the sick feeling in her gut. After a few hours in flight, the vision of the dead outside the base didn't seem real anymore. Instead she imagined finding the streets empty and the base perfectly safe.

Imagining this had worked for the most part, enough that she could finally look forward to this trip. She wanted to find hope again in this settlement Sam wanted to show her and then concentrate on being with him.

"Check it out," Sam said loudly. He pointed out the side window and everyone followed the direction of his finger.

A giant wall stretched out along the hillside as far as Kira could see. There were no mutated bodies wandering the plush green landscape. Trees were blooming beautifully, creating a lush scenery she'd only seen in pictures.

"Wow," she heard Jill whisper the same word going through her mind.

"There's fifty-thousand acres of secure land inside those walls," Sam said. "We've been constructing this place for about eight years, but only finished it six months ago. There are plans to expand, but for now

... this is home, guys."

Kira saw a few darkly dressed guards standing on top of the wall watching them. She couldn't help but smile when they saluted. "I thought you were taking us to the small colony you found in the cave," Kira said, a little confused that she'd never heard of this place. "Are you saying this is where you live?"

Sam chuckled then shrugged. "No ... and yes," he replied. "I'll explain it to you when we arrive at the base. But for now I just want you to enjoy the view. We're only about ten minutes from headquarters."

Kira twisted her lips to the side letting his iffy answer slide for now, only because she didn't want to miss seeing the land from the sky. She gazed out her side window to the hillside below. To see people working in a large tilled field was like something out of the history books. There were green plants sprouting from the ground, and orchards of apple trees. Rows and rows of grapevines grew along the outer edge of a field of corn stalks that looked ready for harvesting.

Kira laughed, excited to see dairy cows of all things grazing in plush green grass. She'd never seen one that she could remember, but basked in the thought that where there were dairy cows, there was milk and possibly even cheese. In a world of despair, life was happening here.

When they finally landed at the base, Kira stretched her legs, thankful to finally have her feet on something solid. It'd been a longer ride than she'd thought it would be. They definitely weren't just outside Oklahoma City. They'd gone farther northwest past the grasslands and into the mountains of Colorado.

The warm breeze from the towering fir trees felt wonderful on her skin. It was quite hot here, though not as bad as the stagnant treeless base she'd left behind. Surrounded by military vehicles coming and going, it was definitely noisier. This place reminded her of the base where she'd stayed overnight before they assigned her to be Claven's assistant.

Here the uniformed men walked by with easy grins. Each one met Sam with a quick salute then went on their way to their destinations as he led his group to theirs.

Kira was surprised to find the small building they walked through was air conditioned. That meant they had a good power source and didn't need to use generators. She wanted to ask Sam about it, but he was on the go toward the back room of the building.

"This is headquarters," he said as he led them through a door into a large empty office.

The room was set up with six desks, one for each member of his crew. That meant Jake's desk was here somewhere, sending a chill clear through her body.

"Jake and the guys are out on a mission right now. They won't be back for a few days, so relax." He chuckled, then puffed out his chest as his gaze went over her head to Pete. "There's a truck waiting outside to take you and Jill up the mountain. We'll catch up with you guys later tonight for dinner."

"Dinner?" Pete said with a grin. "I'm definitely looking forward to that."

Jill giggled when Pete put his arm around her then

led her back outside. It was nice to see Jill relaxed and not as pale as when they'd left. Kira imagined the color had finally returned to her face as well.

Sam sat down on the edge of his desk and gave Kira his full attention. "So how are you holding up?"

She gave him a quick nod. "I'm thrilled to be here, Sir, and very eager to see the rest of the place."

"Good," he replied. "Now go close the door to the office."

Kira shut the door and the moment her hand slid away from the knob, he grasped her wrist. He pulled her close to him, hands sliding around her waist as he stood on his feet.

"I'm glad you came," he spoke softly. He leaned close, within centimeters of a kiss.

"I am too," she replied then leaned back before he could make contact with her lips. "But I'm still wondering about this settlement outside Kansas City. How come you didn't tell them about this place instead?"

He gazed at her for a moment, then sighed. "They want to hear about the good of the world, so that's what I do. I give them what they want to hear."

She folded her arms over her chest. "So your story wasn't true?"

"No, it was true to an extent. Let's just leave it at that. You've already been through enough today." He shrugged then scowled. "You disobeyed my order this morning. I told you not to look down."

She shivered, not wanting to relive that moment—all those dead people surrounding the base. At least she'd been up in the air and not on the ground. And at least she wasn't there anymore, though that would change once this trip was over.

Deciding to forget for now, she pursed her lips as she glanced around at all the empty desks. "So is this where we're staying?"

"No," he replied then opened the door for her. " I have a log cabin just off the lake."

"Oh, a cabin in the woods!" she said excitedly, maybe with a little too much enthusiasm. But how could she not be excited?

She'd lived six years in a box without a window.

Chapter Five

It was two in the afternoon by the time they reached the small log cabin nestled in a tiny clearing between the tallest fir trees Kira had ever seen. A sweet honeysuckle scent blew in the light summer breeze, tickling her senses in a way she'd never experienced. She breathed deeply as she followed Sam up the short flight of stairs to the front door.

It was absolutely refreshing being outside, though still a tad daunting. There were no walls or barbed wire fences around this particular place, and no guards watching closely with heavy weaponry. This cabin seemed like the only place in the world, though Pete was staying in another cabin about a mile down the road. Still, Kira felt she and Sam were all alone, which wasn't a bad thing as long as he stayed close.

The inside of the cabin was spectacular compared to her room at the base. The walls gave off that same alluring woodsy aroma as outside. A bar table separated the kitchen and living room where a small leather couch and recliner sat. And along the wall beside the spiral staircase leading to a loft upstairs was a wood burning stove.

Kira smiled as she gazed at the giant window above the couch. The window took up almost the entire wall letting in the golden rays of sunlight and capturing the most breathtaking view of the mountains in the distance.

"Beautiful, isn't it?" Sam asked from behind her. He placed his hands on her shoulders then leaned her back against his chest. "This place is quite a retreat, but it gets lonely up here."

Kira could definitely see that. She'd be too afraid to stay in this place by herself. If that were the case, she'd have already boarded the windows and stood waiting at the front door with an Uzi in her hands.

"Are you hungry?" Sam asked, turning her around to face him and that gorgeous grin of his.

Kira shook her head and yawned. It'd been such a long day, the most active one she'd had since she could remember. Though she wanted to stay up to explore the small cabin and talk to Sam more, she could barely keep her eyes open.

As if he'd read her mind, he took her by the hand and led her to the spiral staircase. She followed him upstairs to the loft and the queen-sized bed just beneath a large circular window. On each side of the window were smaller rectangular stained glass windows that reflected blue and red streams of sunlight across the bed.

"This is cozy," she said marveling as she plopped herself down on the soft suede cover on the bed. She glanced at the piled clothes on the dresser along the west wall. "How long have you lived here?"

Sam leaned back against the wall and folded his arms over his chest. "I moved here about six years ago to help with boundary watch. We'd just started building the west side wall, so if any infected made it through, I … " He shrugged. "Well I'm sure you understand."

"Thanks for stopping your story there." She lifted her legs onto the bed then slid back to the plain white pillow. "But Sam," she continued as she adjusted the pillow behind her back. She rested her head against the wall as he sat down on the edge of the bed beside her. "This is such a large area of land. Do you think they might still be inside? Maybe they were missed and are still out there wandering in the woods."

"Stop," he said with a chuckle, though she could hear the seriousness in his voice. "With those kinds of thoughts, you're only going to scare yourself. Just relax and enjoy your rest. Besides," he added as he placed his hand over hers. "I haven't seen one infected person since the wall was finished."

Though the very thought of them coming through here at one time made her shiver, she nodded. She slid down until her head rested on the pillow. And the moment her eyes closed, she drifted off to sleep.

She didn't feel Sam leave the bed, nor did she realize she'd actually fallen asleep until she awoke to a darkened room. Light came from downstairs. She heard the wooden floor creak beneath someone's footsteps. With a quick toss of the soft fuzzy brown throw Sam had covered her with, she rose to her feet.

Her stomach growled viciously as she made her

way to the staircase and watched her feet carefully as she stepped down and around until she made it to the bottom floor.

Sam was in the kitchen, a large butcher knife in one hand, a fancy glass of red liquid in the other. As Kira made her way in, she noted the bottle of wine on the counter next to a small pile of freshly chopped vegetables.

Something boiled in a gray pot on the tiny stove. She leaned over to investigate and her eyes lit up in delight. Spaghetti noodles boiled in the water instead of rice. Sam raised the lid on the skillet and showed her the cooked mix of meat.

"It's ground pork," he said. A grin played across his wine-stained lips.

"I thought we were meeting Pete and Jill for dinner," she said as she breathed in the heavenly aroma.

"Pete says Jill's pretty tired," he replied, then finished chopping the tomatoes. He scooped them with a pile of minced onion and garlic into the browned pork. "I told Pete you were resting too, so we've planned for breakfast at the Barnhouse in the morning."

"The Barnhouse?" she asked as he reached into the cabinet for another glass just like his.

He poured red wine from the bottle into the glass then handed it to her. "It's the local cafeteria near the town, well, small marketplace, but it's growing. The Barnyard is kind of like a pancake house from the pre-apoc days. Did your parents ever take you to one when you were young?"

"I'm not sure," she said softly.

He picked up the pot of noodles then poured them out into the colander he'd set inside the sink. Steam rose into the air and fogged the small window above the faucet.

"You were in a car accident with your parents, but don't talk much about it."

"The farthest I can reach with my memory is waking up in a hospital bed on a Navy ship. Sadly, I don't even remember my parents or what they looked like or if they even cared. Jake said they did, but then, he's a stranger to me, too."

"That's sad, Kira," he said drawing her attention to him. He came to stand before her, gazing down into her eyes as he pushed his thumb gently across her cheek. "Does it hurt?"

"Does what hurt?" she replied softly.

"Talking about it."

"No," she replied. She set her glass down on the counter then looked at him again, wanting to reassure him she was just fine, but his lips quickly met hers.

His kiss was gentle, soft as he worked his tongue slowly into her mouth. When he parted from her, she couldn't help but shy away, surprised and yet wonderfully excited.

"I've been wanting to do that all day," he said as he brushed the tip of his nose against hers. He flashed that perfect grin then returned to fixing their dinner.

Kira's legs felt weak. She grabbed her wine glass then found a seat on the stool at the bar table on the other side of the kitchen walkway.

Except for Sam's clang from spooning the

spaghetti out on the plates, it was quiet. Kira turned to the giant window in the living room and looked out into the black of night. She sipped on her wine, downing a little more as she thought of being outside right now. She almost missed the lights of the base, having lived under them for so long, but then she'd definitely rather be here knowing now what awaited in the streets.

Sam made his way around the table, a plate in each hand. He set a dish down in front of her, then sat down on the stool with his and began to eat.

Kira set her glass down and lifted her fork getting a kick out of the noodles stringing below it. She shoveled it into her mouth then sucked in the hanging strands between her lips.

"Oh my," she moaned as she twisted her fork on the plate, grabbing another giant forkful of spaghetti. "This sure beats rice and carrots," she said then washed another bite down with a gulp of red wine. "I feel a little guilty though," she continued blurting her thoughts aloud. "When the people at the base are practically starving. When are they getting evacuated?"

Sam took a swig of his wine, finishing it in one gulp. "It may look like there's a lot of room to accommodate another large group of people, but the fact is there isn't enough room yet. We're just getting started here."

She leaned back surprised. "My God Sam, there's an entire mountainside here with nothing on it but trees."

"Sure, there's plenty of room to build on, but we

don't have the resources to feed a thousand more people. Not yet."

"It's been six years," she said with a shrug. "That's more than enough time for the government to get a handle on the situation."

"And what are you basing that on? You haven't been outside since this began. You can't even remember." He cocked his head to the side. "I'm willing to bet you've never even seen an infected person let alone one up close. What they can do to a living being is beyond comprehension."

She stood, flustered. He'd resorted to bringing them up during their romantic dinner. How did they end up on this discussion anyway? She hated talking about it, even though he was right. Except in her horrifying dreams, the helicopter flight was the first time she could remember seeing one.

"I've witnessed things that would give you nightmares," he continued, picking up his empty glass as he stood. He maneuvered around the table then went straight to the wine bottle. As he poured himself another glass, he glanced back at her. "They're fast, Kira. People call them the walking dead but that's bull. You can be twenty yards away and they'd be on top of you in a matter of seconds."

"I don't want to talk about it anymore." She scowled as she sat back down on the bar stool.

Sam refilled her glass then slammed the bottle down on the counter making her jump. He slid her plate to the side then leaned over until he was face to face with her.

"I've seen them dig into a person's stomach with

their bare hands, pulling out innards, eating … "

"Shut up!" she screamed, immediate tears in her eyes. She covered her ears with her hands as she slid off the barstool. The vision of what he'd said played in her mind like a horror movie making her ill as she sunk down in the living room recliner and leaned over her knees.

"Kira," Sam said as he knelt before her. He grasped her wrists and gently pulled her hands from her ears. "I'm sorry honey, but this is reality. You keep running from the truth, from your memories. You need to see the world for what it really is."

She looked at him through blurry eyes. "I didn't know there were so many of them on the other side of the wall," she whispered, shaking her head. "I've never even looked because I was too scared to see it. I didn't want to believe …"

"It's okay," he said taking her face in his hands.

She pulled from his touch. "It's not okay," she retorted, remembering she would have to face it again very soon. "It's not okay because I'm petrified. I'm supposed to be a soldier, but I … I don't want to go back to my post. I'm ashamed."

"Don't be." He sat back on his heels. "To be honest, I never planned on taking you back."

"What?" She wiped her cheeks with the back of her hand.

"I was going to suggest you stay here, somewhere in the community. You'd be close to me. You could have your own room at the resort, or we could make arrangements to find you a cabin. And then … there's also the option of moving in here with me."

She suddenly fell into his arms, practically knocking him over to the floor in the process. Excitement loomed over her at the mere thought of being here with him, and more so to never have to go back to the base again.

Realizing she'd thrown her body at him, she leaned back and gazed into his eyes, feeling a little embarrassed at first. With her legs wrapped around his waist and arms still holding on to his neck, the excitement of staying here at the cabin with him turned into a longing to be with him now.

He raised his hand to her face, touching her gently. She shivered as he traced her jaw-line with his thumb. She could see it in his eyes, the hunger for her.

"All these years, Kira, I never meant to be in your life," he said leaning close, stealing a kiss from her lips. "Not like this anyway," he added, pressing his lips to hers once more before he moved her off his lap and into the floor. He stood and faced the dark window, hands pinching his sides.

In a flash she was up, arms wrapped around his torso. With her cheek pressed against his chest, she could hear his heart beating in perfect rhythm. His shirt was soft on her fingertips as she pulled the garment up and slid her hands up inside. His skin was warm as she raked her nails softly up and down his back.

His fingers gently pushed through her hair. "I'm here for you, Kira," he spoke softly in her ear. "I'll never hurt you again."

She took him by the hand and led him up the

spiral stairs. When she reached the bed she pulled off her shirt then unclasped her bra in back. He watched as she slid the white straps down her arms. His eyes never moved from her as she let the undergarment fall to the floor at her feet.

She shoved her cargo pants down then kicked them to the side. Now standing naked before him, she waited for him to make his move. But that gorgeous grin of his spread across his face as he leaned back on his heels and inspected her body with an arched brow.

The temperature of the room seemed to suddenly drop. She shivered, glancing down to see if there was something wrong, but couldn't find anything that could possibly amuse him.

"What's is it?" she asked with a shrug. "Oh," she breathed, remembering the large scar on the back of her leg. He was probably staring at that unsightly thing, though she couldn't figure out why he'd laugh about it.

She turned her leg and glanced down, showing him the entire deep scar from the back of her ankle to her knee. "I've never shown it to anyone but you. Well, Pete's seen it, but only because he hangs out in my room some nights, as a friend of course."

Sam chuckled, then mm'ed. "I wasn't looking at your scar, honey. I was looking at you. You're so beautiful—as pretty as the day we met."

As he moved toward her he pulled off his shirt then tossed it into the floor. She marveled at his perfectly toned chest, spotting a few of his own nasty looking scars. He noticed her gaze settled on the four long jagged marks above his right peck. "A fight with a grizzly," he answered before she could ask. He slid off his pants then tossed them into the floor beside hers.

She swallowed hard as he moved closer. "A grizzly?" She wanted to hear more about it, but her eyes wandered to the small oval shape on his left shoulder. "Is that a bullet wound?"

He nodded as he reached out and touched her neck. His hands gently glided down, tickling her slightly when he palmed her breasts. She moaned when his fingers massaged her erect nipples, pinching ever so gently. Her skin rose when his right hand slid down over her stomach to the sensitive spot between her thighs. He briefly dipped his finger inside her, sending fire screaming through her veins and a gasp from her mouth.

"You like that?" he whispered, his lips against her ear. She nodded as his forefinger moved, tangling slightly in the short hairs. She shivered as he ran his lips down her neck then stopped to flick his tongue over her tingling nipple.

"Oh Sam," she moaned, grasping his head in her hands. "If you keep this up, I won't last long enough to get you into the bed."

She slid her hands over his broad shoulders as he continued licking from one nipple to the other. About to burst, she shoved him away, arm stretched out before her to stop him from advancing on her again.

"It's okay Kira," he said with a short laugh, moving forward until her palm touched his chest. "Let me please you."

"I need to catch my breath first," she demanded, concentrating on dousing the tension inside her. It was difficult, biting back the ache to let him continue touching her. "Just go lie down Sam."

At first he hesitated. But when she pointed at the bed, he obeyed by tossing his body down, causing the springs in the mattress to squeak. He put his hands behind his head and smiled at her, looking rather sexy and quite rebellious.

Finally in control, Kira crawled onto the bed. Wanting him to feel the same way she did a moment ago, she ran her tongue along the length of his erection. He groaned when she took his hard tip into her mouth then gently pulled on his smooth skin. He buried his fingers in her hair, stroking her head. "This isn't fair, you know," he said raising up. He curled his arm around her waist then effortlessly pulled her around until she was straddling his chest. "That's more like it."

Kira wasn't sure she was comfortable like this. She'd never been in this position before, though it seemed he had experience. For a moment she was a little hesitant until she felt his warm tongue slide against the sensitive knob near her opening.

Her body shuddered. She pulled her mouth away from him unable to hold in the gasping breath.

"No, no," she whispered then moaned. This felt so good ... too good to let him continue. She had to pull away otherwise this wondrous rendezvous would end quickly.

"No what?" he said, his mouth again against her

opening. His hands slid over her backside, massaging, pinching her flesh. It tickled. Then when he stuck his tongue inside her, she quickly moved forward and away.

She turned around then sat down on the bed beside him gazing at him, panting for breath with, she knew, the most ridiculous grin on her face. "I'm too shy for that," she confessed, about to explode from the pleasure.

"Don't be." He growled as he grasped her hand. He pulled her back over to him then shoved her down on the bed. "I like exploring your body," he said as he wedged between her knees, running his hands up her legs, grasping and pulling her closer to him. "I didn't get to play with you last night," he continued. "Our first time together should have been more like this."

He grasped his shaft in his hand. Sliding his tip against her sensitive knob, she moaned in delight. He dipped the head inside her then pulled it back out again.

"You're teasing me," she whimpered, desperate to feel him deep inside. He teased her again, swirling his head around in circles along the lip before pulling it back out again. She arched her back, raising her hips against him. "Please," she pleaded, reaching for him. "I need to feel you inside me now."

Thankfully, he complied as he moved his body over hers. His mouth found hers as he dipped his tip in once again then began to move against her. It was leisurely at first, a little bit of a tease as he worked his way in with slow movements of his hips.

She arched, feeling his chest rub against her erect

nipples. His hands massaged the soft skin of her thighs, squeezing as he moved and breathed. Then he sat up on his knees. He lifted her legs over his broad shoulders and looked down watching as he penetrated her.

"You're so wet," he said with a grunt, breathing through his mouth as he thrust a little faster.

Kira pulled her head up until she could see his shaft appear then disappear inside her. He pulled it out all the way, swirled it around her sensitive knob, then quickly pushed it back in.

That was all she could stand. Whether he was ready or not, she'd reached her threshold, immediately going into a fit of moans. His breath quickened as her body shuddered, insides clamping down on him. She turned her gaze to his, crying out as he lifted her body against him and held tight around his neck.

"Sam," she cried out, pressing down hard against his hips as he thrust upward.

He silenced her with a kiss as he fell back on the bed, holding her against him, in as deep as he could go. She felt his shaft pulse against her walls as he released his warmth, thrusting with a few more urgent thrusts until his body finally began to calm.

Kira breathed deeply, quite satisfied. She began to laugh, stretching her body out over his. "I don't think I've ever felt quite like this before," she said, delighted.

Sam puffed out a few more breaths as he stared at the ceiling. And when he finally looked at her, he flashed that grin she so loved to see.

She didn't want to move away from him. Her smile broadened as she leaned her face against his chest, listening to the thumping of his heart.

"Could we stay here forever lying together in each other's arms?" she said in a breathy whisper.

"I wish we could, but I have to go back to headquarters in the morning," Sam replied, interrupting the heartbeats she'd begun to count. "Pete'll bring you back here after breakfast."

She moved off of him but stayed close to his side. A chill caught her skin at the thought of being here alone.

"I'll come with you," she replied coolly, wondering if Jake would be there too.

He chuckled as he stroked his fingers across her back. "I figured you'd want to accompany me, but I'd rather you stayed here. In fact, I think it's best if you stayed with Pete and Jill while I'm gone. I might not be back for a few days."

"What do you mean a few days?" she asked, her throat clenched in worry. Just the mere thought of him going out there now frightened her. "I don't want you to leave," she pleaded. "I want you here with me."

He leaned on his elbow and gazed at her, studying her face as she solemnly looked at him. "I don't want to leave you either. But, honey, you know I can't always be here," he said in a soothing tenor. "I'm still a soldier."

She sighed knowing that all too well. She was a soldier too, but was ducking out of her responsibilities because she was a coward. She felt terribly guilty for not going back to the Oklahoma base. There were so many dead surrounding it, pounding on the walls, desperately wanting in. And all those people she'd be letting down would suffer if they somehow broke through.

"Why haven't you and your team taken care of the base?" she asked. It was a logical question, one she was quite curious of hearing the answer to.

His brows lowered for a moment, but relaxed when he returned his attention on her. "That problem is being dealt with. So don't worry anymore about it, okay?"

She nodded, thankful something was being done, evacuations hopefully. When he leaned back on the bed, she folded her arms over his chest. She leaned her chin on her forearm thinking about everything that had happened in the past two days.

"Tell me more about these super powers you have."

"Didn't you learn enough the other night? I nearly killed you because of them."

"I was inebriated, though I do sort of recollect an intense burning when your body was on fire. You're just too hot to handle Sam Riles." But when he didn't follow along with her attempt to make it into something lighter than it was, she shrugged. "I'm still alive. So stop beating yourself up about it."

"That was the first and last time I'll use my powers while I'm drunk," he said, stroking the back of her hand with his fingers. "I always have superior control over my strength."

"Show me," she said, hoping he'd do something incredible. "Wow me."

"Wow you?" he said then laughed.

Kira suddenly felt something creeping up her

legs. She glanced down to find the blanket moving slowly up over her by itself. Her skin broke out in goose bumps as the edge of the cover stopped midway up her back, then slid back down exposing her bare behind.

Her eyes widened when she turned her attention on Sam. It was difficult to believe that he'd actually moved the blanket with his mind. But she'd seen it with her own eyes.

"What else can you do?" she said in awe.

"I'd tell you," he replied. "But I don't want to scare you."

"Oh, come on," she pleaded, grinning profusely. "You should know by now that you can't frighten me away."

If you only knew, Kira, just how frightening I can be.

She'd heard him speak the words, but never saw his lips move.

"Are you serious?" she blurted as she rose to her knees gawking down at him. "You're telepathic!"

She remembered hearing his voice in the alley, like an echo inside her head. She'd dismissed it as delusions from having too much to drink. But this was exciting, though also a bit unnerving. She wondered if he could read her mind, and how often he'd done it without her knowing.

"Except the one night in the alley, and right now, I've never read your mind," he answered her questions aloud. "I can do it easily with people I have connections with, good friends, lovers. But with others it takes a lot more concentration."

She gently bounced up and down on her knees, delighted he'd done it again. She wanted to find out what other extraordinary things he could do, but really wanted to play these mind tricks a little longer.

"Okay, tell me what I'm thinking," she said as she closed her eyes and thought about the mountain view outside the window.

"You should see the mountains in winter covered in snow. Beautiful," he said. *But not as beautiful as you.*

"That was too easy," she said with a laugh, loving his voice inside her head. "Okay, let me think of something else." She closed her eyes and thought of their lovemaking a little while ago. Seeing him dive in and out of her, and how much that little bit turned her on, she felt her insides churn.

"Oh my," he said immediately sitting up. His mouth met hers but only briefly before he pulled away. "Here's another trick of mine," he whispered in her ear.

He leaned her back on the bed bending her knees up and spreading her feet wide. She dug her toes into the blanket as she laid there fully exposed to him, accepting him between her legs.

He slid his hand over her face then smiled. *Close your eyes*, she heard him say in her mind.

The moment her eyes fluttered shut she found herself on a sandy beach. A warm breeze played in her hair as she looked out across a calm ocean into a rich golden sunset.

"Sam," she whispered finding him standing beside her on the beach. It seemed so real and yet surreal at the same time. "This is beautiful!"

"This was my parents vacation home in Hawaii," he said, turning her around to see the two-story villa with the beach side wall made of nothing but windows. "I've often dreamed of coming back here, setting up my own little security system, then hopefully leading a full happy life with someone I love."

Tears sprung to her eyes when she opened them. He'd shown her his dreams, letting her see that not everything about him was soldier. She pulled him close, guiding his hips between her legs. "Someday you'll make it there," she whispered as he gently pushed inside her.

He kissed her mouth then replied, "Someday, Kira, we will make it there."

Chapter Six

Kira's day started off on the wrong side of the bed. Her cargo pants had somehow gotten snagged on the bottom of the dresser in the loft. When she tugged on them, they tore up the back of the right leg. She rarely used profanity, never really cared to hear it either, but this little incident made her say a few choice words. It wasn't that she was planning on wearing her cargos today anyway, but she hadn't brought very many clothes.

She hopped into her only pair of jeans then met Sam downstairs in the kitchen where he offered her a cup of coffee. She miscalculated the amount in her cup and tipped it too far, spilling the hot liquid down the front of her favorite blue tank top. A few more choice words spilled past her wet lips as coffee splashed out onto her lap, staining her jeans with prominent wet brown spots. The only thing she had left to wear now was her long white T-shirt that doubled as her sleep wear.

Sam cheered her up with a little rendezvous in

the shower. He'd stood at her back lathering her hair with his gentle hands. Her body tingled from the bubbly soap he massaged onto her skin, paying close attention to her breasts.

She would've lathered his chest, but he'd bent his knees and slid into her from behind. She'd never had sex quite like it, feeling his hard body slide against her back. His arms were around her waist, fingers working through the wet hair between her thighs. He'd even created a soft light around them, warming her insides as he thrust until they finally came together.

After that, the day looked brighter. It didn't matter what she wore now. Even though that unsightly red scar on her leg showed below the hem of the white shirt, she had the confidence to take on the world as long as Sam was with her.

She couldn't get enough of him, especially knowing he might be gone for a few days, out there … with them. He'd fought the living dead for years without incident. And though she'd worried about him before, now it was almost unbearable. She couldn't lose him now. And as they headed down the mountain road, the thought of him leaving made her ill.

"Stop the vehicle," she said, touching his hand.

He pulled the Hummer over to the side of the dirt road, in the shade just beneath the tall fir trees. For a moment they sat in silence, just the sound of the engine rumbling and cool air blowing gently through the vents.

"What is it?" he finally asked breaking the silence.

When she looked at him, her heart stung. What if this was their final moment together? What if he never came back to her? What if ... she went back to her duties at the base like a good soldier would do? She could stay busy there, at least until they were evacuated.

"Kira," he demanded gathering her immediate attention.

Tears welled in her eyes as she looked at him, memorizing his face, the way his blue eyes stood out as he looked at her. It was almost as if she could reach out to touch him and he'd already be gone. She could barely stand the ache in her heart.

He reached across the space between the seats and palmed her face. "What's going on in that beautiful head of yours?"

"You can read my mind, can't you?" she said with a sniffle, then tried to laugh it off though her body trembled.

"I could. But like I told you last night, I won't. I'd rather hear whatever it is you're thinking about come from your mouth."

She sighed as she stared out the windshield, over the hood of the Hummer, down the straight stretch of shadowed dirt road. Her thoughts terrified her, but she knew what she had to do. She had to be a brave soldier.

"I want to go back to the base," she finally said. Her voice wavered slightly, but she cleared her throat. She threw him a confident smile as he gazed at her with lowered brows. "You do your job every day out there in the open where it's unsafe. As scared as it makes me, I need to go back and be a soldier. If I stay here, people will think I'm a coward. And I'll feel like I've deserted them."

"No, Kira," he said shaking his head. "Nobody will ever think you're a coward."

"Come on, Sam. You know that's not true."

He gave a short sigh, turning his gaze on the road in front of them. She wished she could read his mind. And if he read hers at the moment, he'd hear her voice softly whispering how much he meant to her ... how much she loved him. It hurt to love him knowing she'd have to say goodbye for a little while, at least until the base was evacuated. Until then, she'd stand her post and try not to think about the dead outside the walls desperate to get in.

"We need to go back to how things were before you brought me here," she continued catching his eyes in hers. "It's not fair for me to be here when everyone else I know is stuck in that ... camp. So please, take me back."

"That's very admirable of you, Kira," he muttered as he shifted the Hummer into drive and pulled back out on the road. "We'll see what happens when you see the rest of this place."

After they picked up an eager Pete and Jill, they headed down the mountain for breakfast. Sam parked the Hummer off to the side of the wide dirt road where they all got out.

Kira took everything in as they walked along the flat stretch of land Sam had called the Marketplace, where people traded fresh produce and clothing with each other. There was a cart of shoes and dresses hanging from a multicolored tent. Some had tags on them, the same kind of tags on the shoes Sam brought her on her birthday, the same ones she wore now.

Sam took her hand as they walked toward a group of buildings at the end of the road where children ran, laughing as they played a game of tag. "That's the school," Sam told her with a squeeze of his hand.

Kira couldn't remember the last time she'd seen children. She glanced back when they passed, wishing she had time to stop and watch them for awhile. Their laughter was an encouraging sound that meant no matter how troubled the world was, life kept going ... here at least.

Sam led them into an open building to a room filled with people eating and laughing with each other. In the center of the room were three long tables with lighted canopies displaying a splendid buffet of all kinds of food. Kira saw Pete's eyes light up.

"We're only allowed to go once," Sam reminded Pete as he grabbed two plates at the end of the table. "That's my brother ... the glutton," he added as he handed Kira an empty white plate.

Kira followed Sam down the line in awe. She couldn't believe the food. There were strawberries and kiwi, not the canned kind either. They were fresh and colorful on her bright white plate. She arranged them on the side to make room for pancakes made with real flour and a side of perfect scrambled eggs.

"Sir," a young dark-haired man said as he came to stand at the end of the line. He tossed Sam a quick salute then lowered his hands to his sides. "You're wanted at Headquarters."

Sam gave him a quick nod then handed Kira his plate. "I won't be long," he said. She noticed a little worry in those beautiful blue eyes. "Go ahead and eat." He gave her a quick peck on the lips then left before she could say anything.

Pete was almost in tears as he ate. His plate was overloaded with practically everything on the bar while Jill and Kira's plates had significantly less.

"You're such a pig," Kira said snorting out a short laugh through her nose. It'd felt like forever since she'd given Pete a hard time. "There are other people here that need to eat, you know."

Jill giggled at her comment, but Pete glared. He finished chewing whatever it was he chewed on, then slowly stuffed an entire pancake in his mouth. He acted as if he'd found heaven, letting the syrup purposely drip over his lips.

"You really are a glutton," Kira said as Jill wiped the syrup from his chin with a napkin, looking rather disgusted.

"Where'd Sam go?" Pete asked after washing the monster bite down with orange juice.

Kira briefly gazed at the door. "They called him to Headquarters."

She hadn't expected Sam to leave so soon, though she should have known. He and Jake were important people, super-soldiers like the rest of his crew. Funny she hadn't thought of the rest of them until just this moment. If Jake was at headquarters now, she wanted to see him.

She picked up Sam's plate and left the table. Eager

to get to Sam, she hurried through the small crowd of people leading toward the base on the other side of the field. She recognized the building as the same one they'd come to the previous day.

She maneuvered through heavy vehicle traffic wondering what was going on. It looked like a rally of troops preparing to move out to a war zone.

She took the short flight of steps to the door on the main building and went in. The place was hopping with camouflaged soldiers, some with heavy guns in their hands. There was a lot of chatter, so concentrating on one voice was hard as she made her way through the crowded room toward the office door.

The door was closed. She could see movement on the other side of the cloudy window but couldn't see who it was. She heard a few angry muffled shouts, then sudden silence. The door opened causing her to jump. Sam stood there, hand on the knob, glaring. She swallowed the lump in her throat hoping she hadn't stepped out of line by coming here and interrupting his meeting.

He grabbed her arm, pulled her into the room, then shut the door. She smiled when she saw the crew sitting at their desks grinning back at her though seemingly a bit forced, but she'd obviously walked into an argument she wasn't supposed to be in the middle of.

She noticed the guy standing in the back of the room facing the large window overlooking the forest. She recognized him, even from the back. With the short dark brown hair and unmistakable stance, weight always shifted to his right leg— Jake.

"Hello," she said to burly Kyle, Maurey, and Jayson; the three other soldiers who worked beside Jake and Sam. She waved a short wave with the breakfast plate, then her gaze went straight to Jake's back. She set Sam's plate of food down on the desk as each of them replied with a cold nod.

"Kira," Jake said turning around. He offered her a smug grin, one she didn't think she'd ever see again. Then a sudden memory of when they were kids swarmed through her mind.

Jake was twelve-years-old and she was just six. As rambunctious as he was with the neighborhood boys, he always took care of her, standing up to his friends when they picked on her. It was strange to be thinking of this now, as if he'd put the memory in her head. Or, quite possibly, this strange meeting with him made her remember it.

"Jake." Her voice cracked a little, but she cleared her throat to continue. "How've you been?"

He glanced at Sam then back to her. "Good. We're in a bit of a discussion right now," he added as he strode toward her. He took hold of her arm and escorted her toward the door. "Could you excuse us?"

"She has the right to know what's going on," Sam interrupted as he grasped her other arm, stopping Jake from kicking her out of the room.

Kira was stunned. Caught between two people she cared about who were not seeing eye-to-eye and lethal super-soldiers at that. It was a little unnerving. But if she had a right to know about whatever they squabbled about, just like Sam said, she was going to stay and listen.

Jake suddenly slammed his fist down on the desk causing a large crack down the center of it. "I'm your superior, Sam. What I say is final."

"She'll find out anyway. We should tell her now and get it over with," Sam replied calmly.

"What's going on?"

"It's okay, honey," Sam replied as he palmed the back of her head and nudged her toward the door. "Why don't you just go back to the Marketplace. I'll join you in a little while."

"No," she argued pulling away from him. "Not until you tell me what's going on."

She looked at Jake hoping he would talk, but he couldn't take his angry eyes off Sam. Blue flames danced over him, just like they had over Sam's body in the alley that night.

"Calm down, Jake," Kyle said, his voice gruff and fierce. He immediately stood up followed by Jayson and Maurey who'd sat quietly at their desks until now. Kyle towered over everyone by a good foot and a half, but even he hesitated reaching for Jake.

"You've been screwing my sister?" Jake shouted as he lunged for Sam only to be stopped by Kyle's large hands. Jayson and Maurey grabbed Jake by the arms and shoved him out the office door into the crowded room.

Kira felt warmth rush to her face as they left her alone in the room with Sam. Embarrassed and confused, she sat down in the first chair she found and hid her face in her hands.

"Jake read my mind, didn't he?" she said watching

through her fingers as Sam sat down on the edge of the desk.

"No. He read mine the moment you walked in here."

She looked up at him as he looked down at her. He grinned, though it was definitely not the sweet, lovable smirk she loved to see. It was solemn as if he knew he had some explaining to do and it was going to be rough.

"What argument did I walk in the middle of?" she pleaded.

Sam sighed then nodded. He momentarily pinched the crease between his eyes then turned his attention on her. "The military's getting ready to nuke the base. Jake didn't want you to know, but I didn't want to keep it from you."

Kira was dumbfounded, but somehow knew the military would do such a thing. "That makes sense," she said. "After seeing all the dead people outside the base desperate to get in, it's really the only option." She drew in a relieving breath. "At least everyone will finally be evacuated." Seeing Sam frown as he gazed at his hand resting on his lap, it dawned on her what the argument between him and Jake was really about. "Oh no, no ... " she continued, tears immediately welling in her eyes. "Please tell me they're evacuating all those people."

"Kira," he said as she quickly stood. He turned his pleading eyes to hers. "The outer walls are crumbling. That's why I came to get you."

"I don't want to hear it!" she cried.

"Look," he said placing his hands on her shoulders.

"The guys spent the night evacuating as many as they can. Casualties will be very low ... "

"That's not good enough," she said in a breath, struggling with the urge to break down into full-blown crying. "I know so many of those people. I logged them in when they had nowhere else to go, when they were fighting for their lives. How can I stand back and do nothing?"

"You have no other choice," he said.

"How many people will die?"

"I'm not sure. Fifty, maybe sixty people ... I just don't know."

She immediately turned away from him, feeling his warm hands slide away from her shoulders. In tears she hurried out the office door and shoved her way through the crowded building, quickly passing her brother and ignoring him when he called her name. She ran out the door only to be stopped by a tall lean body, one she knew all too well. His gray hair and leathery skin was prominent in the sunshine, so much he looked as if he'd aged ten years since she'd seen him just a few days ago at the base.

"Commander Claven?" she said as she wiped tears from her eyes. "What are you doing here?"

He growled. "Evacuated. They're nuking the damned place tonight."

"They didn't get everyone out! We have to go back and save them."

"Won't happen, Spence. It's just a matter of time before the dead tear down the walls."

Her superior stood before her scowling. It took her a moment to realize she hadn't issued the proper greeting. She bent her arm forward, but he grasped her hand and shoved it away before she could salute.

"Casualties of war," he retorted, mouth frowning. He puckered his nose as he stared unflinchingly into her eyes. "Look, Spence, don't get all flustered and scared because you think everyone's gonna die. We knew someday those walls would crumble."

"S … sir?" she stammered unable to comprehend why he was saying such horrible things, why he of all people wouldn't do what it took to get the innocent civilians out of there before they bombed the place.

"Take a look, Spence," he said, motioning with a nod for her to look at a group of heavily armed soldiers loading wooden crates into a chopper. "They're going to the base to set up ground work for the nuke job."

"And while they're doing that, the other choppers could be evacuating people."

"Don't give me crap!" he shouted in her face. He must have seen more tears welling in her eyes, because he backed off a step. His face lightened to a straight-lipped purse. "You've been with me for six years. Now I'm not one for giving compliments, but you've stuck with me, which is a feat not many soldiers can live up to. You're special Spence. That's why you've got to think like a real soldier now. " He gave her a quick wink then tossed a nod to one of the empty passenger helicopters. "Don't run away with your tail between your legs. Step up to the plate …"

"All right, all right," she said with a sniffle. "I get it, Commander."

"Good luck," he said sternly. "Be the soldier I

know you can be. Be a hero, one everyone in that God forsaken base can look up to and say, 'she saved our lives." He placed his hand on her shoulder then gently squeezed. "I'm proud of you Kira. I've come to think of you like a daughter. So be careful." He looked at the hands on his large silver watch then took it off and handed it to her. "You have ten hours to get in, evacuate as many people as you can, then get at least ten miles from the city. The farther away the better."

Kira looked again at the soldiers in the freight chopper. As it rose from the ground, Claven walked away heading for the main building. He was right. She needed to suck it up and do whatever she could for the good of the people at the base. She'd ignore the dead outside, and the fact the place was about to be annihilated, or overrun as fate would have it, as she landed near the warehouse.

Kira hurried toward the empty chopper, careful not to catch any unwanted attention. It'd been a long time since she'd flown one of these beasts that seated at least twenty people. Hopefully it was just like riding a bicycle as she hopped up into the pilot's seat and immediately began powering it up.

Thankfully nobody noticed at first, possibly thinking it was just another group of soldiers heading out to the battlefield. Then Sam walked out the headquarters' door. His head turned this way then that, most likely searching for her. She tried not to think about what she was doing as she pulled on the throttle sending the chopper forward instead of upward. Sam immediately turned her way. He ran toward her, shouting for her to stop.

"Damn," she whispered. Realizing her mistake, she quickly set the throttle back in position then lifted the bird into the sky. She looked down to find the base flooding with soldiers. They aimed their weapons but was told by a familiar dark-headed man to stand down.

"Thanks Jake," she whispered as she flew the chopper out over the base toward the mountain range.

She'd gotten away. Nobody would stop her from getting the people off the base. The only thing she had to worry about now was to find a safe place far enough away from the blast site until she got every last one of them out.

Chapter Seven

After only a few minutes of flying, Kira finally had the hang of it. Her training came back to her the moment she lifted the helicopter into the sky. She'd taken courses during her initial military training way before the car accident with her parents. She'd even graduated as a top-rate pilot cashing in on an odd title by her superiors. They'd called her "Friles."

The name was a puzzle, but it was no doubt a memory. Strange she'd only recently began to remember bits and pieces, as if this new place had healing powers. The scenery was indeed magical, serene enough that she'd let down her guard just long enough to allow those fragments of her life to come back. Now if only she could remember the rest of her life, including the accident itself, she might find a little more courage in what she was doing.

Jake had continually refused to tell her about the accident, convincing her it'd be too traumatic for her to hear, though she knew she could handle it now. She was a soldier again, willing to put her life on the line for the people she cared about. It was all because of Sam. He'd given her reason to think better of herself, to find strength she'd buried away for so long. He'd given her hope.

"Turn the damn chopper around," she heard Sam shout as he slid into the co-pilot's seat. Not expecting him, or anyone to be on this flight with her, she jumped about a mile off the seat. Her heart practically popped out of her chest. "Kira, what the hell are you trying to prove?"

She glared as she let out a short breath. "I'm not trying to prove anything, Sam!" she yelled wondering how in the world he got on this flight without her knowing. "I'm getting those innocent people off the base before the military destroys it."

"There's no time for evacuation," he replied. "I know you're upset. But there's nothing we can do."

"Don't try to stop me," she said wishing the chopper would go a little faster. "If you don't like what I'm doing, then you should get off the flight now. I'll do this myself."

For a moment he stared at her, inspecting her face, possibly reading her mind. If he was searching for a way to convince her to go back, he wouldn't find it. But then, he didn't need to read her mind to see that she was scared to death.

Her hands trembled as she gripped the throttle tightly. As much as she'd love to go back to the base where it was safe, she just couldn't do it. Not when there were so many innocent people to save.

"You're willing to die for them?" Sam asked, a curious expression on his face.

She caught his eyes in hers. For a brief moment she gazed into those gorgeous blue gems. He didn't flinch, just stared as he waited for her answer.

Tears sprung to her eyes, but not because of the fear of dying, not over the possibility of her nightmare coming true. Even with the image of her standing in the middle of a horde of zombies ready to tear her body apart, she had no doubt in her mind what her answer would be. She would indeed die for them.

Sam immediately leaned over her. He grabbed the communications headset above the pilot side door then placed it over her head and turned it on. After he put on his headset, he looked at her.

"There's an airport in Kingfisher. We'll need to make a stop there to make sure it's safe before we start evacuating."

Kira shivered wishing the entire military was backing her on this. It was ridiculous that they couldn't, or wouldn't do this when they had all the necessary resources. It didn't really make sense.

"Are you all right?" Sam asked. "We can always turn around. Nobody would blame you if you did."

"I'm fine Sam," she replied angrily. "I'm not turning back. So don't say it again."

He nodded then placed his hand on her shoulder and gave her a gentle squeeze. "Then we are right behind you."

"We?" she asked taking her eyes off the sky for a moment to look at him. When he motioned with a quick nod toward the back of the chopper, she glanced back to find Kyle sitting in the seat right behind Sam. He smiled as he took his left hand off the large assault rifle standing up on his right leg. He grabbed the belt of giant shells strapped around his shoulder then gave it a quick jerk. And when he released it from his grasp, he waved at her.

A major rush of enthusiasm worked its way through her entire body. She'd met Kyle a few times before. He was an awesome sight with his massive, muscular body. With his head shaved and dark goatee, he was the epitome of the gun toting, trigger-happy, obnoxious type. But the guy wore his admiration for the job on his sleeve. His sense of humor went above and beyond anyone she'd ever met, especially when it came to killing them. He'd even made it into a game, keeping track of how many heads he'd blown off. As demented as that was, Kira respected him for it. And if there was anyone else besides Sam that she'd want backing her, it was definitely Kyle.

It was eleven AM by the time they reached the Kingfisher airport. From the air it looked like an abandoned station, one that had possibly been used as a safe control point at one time. The fence around one of the hangars was torn down in several areas. She didn't want to imagine what happened to the people inside, though she knew not many had survived, if any at all.

Sam pointed toward the north end of the hangar near the airstrip. "Land there."

Kira did as he instructed. It wasn't a perfectly smooth transition from air to land, but she impressed herself how well it went. If she remembered correctly, she was never that great at landing these things.

"Keep the engine running," Sam told her as Kyle

handed him an assault rifle. He inspected it, making sure it was loaded and ready. "Stay here. If you see anyone else but Kyle or me coming toward you, get this thing back in the air."

Kira slid the headset off and set it in her lap. "I'm going with you."

Sam shook his head. "You're staying here."

She opened her mouth to argue more, but his voice entered her thoughts. *I don't want you to see the dead bodies inside. Just listen to me for once!*

"Just listen to me, Kira," he pleaded. "I'll be back as soon as it's safe."

He hopped out of the chopper. Kyle followed. Kira couldn't help but shiver, thinking of Sam's thoughts. Sure there were probably bodies strung out through the hangar, casualties from when the dead breeched this poorly constructed safety area. But why would Sam put thoughts like that into her head?

Whatever the case, she knew he was right. She didn't want to see bodies ripped to shreds, or possibly even an undead or two still walking around. Sam and Kyle would take care of it then let her know when it was all right to come in.

She looked at Commander Claven's watch loosely hanging around her wrist. They only had six hours left until they dropped the bomb on Oklahoma City. She couldn't imagine how devastating it'd be for the people that had lived there before. All their belongings would be obliterated, memories of when life was normal, gone within a blink of an eye. If the threat of the world were to finally end, those poor souls wouldn't have a home to go back to.

Kira sighed as she scanned the open area. No movement. Thank God there wasn't any of those things here, but neither were there signs of life.

"Come on, Sam," she whispered scoping the open hangar door. Then finally, she caught sight of him jogging toward her. He opened the door on her side then motioned for her to scoot over into the co-pilot's seat.

Not that she didn't enjoy piloting this vessel, but she was glad he was taking over. It'd give her a chance to plan the evacuation. Where was she going to begin? Hopefully, this plan wasn't going to instill chaos.

"Kyle's staying to lock down the hangar," Sam said as he lifted the chopper into the sky.

When Kira nodded that she understood, the radio signaled. Sam tossed her a quick glance as if warning her that their mission was about to fail. Kira knew exactly who it was before he said anything.

"Kira, you know you can't save them all," Jake announced. She could hear the frustration in his analog voice. "Sam, I just got a call from Kyle. He's working on the perimeter and should have the fence up before you bring in the first group of civilians. We're on our way down there now."

"What's your ETA?" Sam asked checking his silver digital watch that looked very similar to the watch Claven gave her.

"Approximately three hours." Jake gave a long sigh, one Kira was sure he wanted everyone to hear. "Damn it, Sam, if you get my sister killed, I'll personally kill you. I don't care how long we've known each other. I will put a bullet in your brain if anything happens to her."

A breath rolled past Kira's lips as a memory of her childhood suddenly hit her. A young boy with sandy blond hair and blue eyes stood out against the bright green of her parents front lawn. He knelt beside her as she sat in the soft grass, tears rolling down her cheeks. The boy held the body of her favorite doll in one hand and the head of it in the other.

"I won't let them do it again," the young boy said. "I swear on my life. I'll always be here to protect you. I'm here, Kira. I've always been here."

Kira covered her mouth with her hand. This was a vision of Sam as the young boy who lived across the street from her family. He was Jake's best friend and her protector from the mean neighborhood boys. How could she have forgotten?

"You know me, Jake," Sam replied tossing her quick glance. "I'd die before I see anything happen to her."

When the call ended, Kira grabbed hold of Sam's hand. She held on as tight as she could, as if letting go of him would somehow make him go away. Though this memory was only a small piece of her past, she knew in her heart that she'd loved this man her entire life, never knowing just how much he truly meant to her until this very moment. If only she'd remembered during their time together in the cabin, she would've confessed everything to him. She would've told him how much she loved him.

As the chopper descended slowly toward the

ground at the base, Kira was careful not to look down along the boundaries where the dead pounded on the towering barricade. She noticed a few of the guards were still standing on the tower, guns aimed toward the opposite side of the wall. Shots were fired.

Two suited officers stood at the gate, including her friend Frances. She knew he'd die before he left his post, a soldier through and through, as the rest of the military side of the base was empty. She couldn't believe they'd evacuate all the soldiers and not the civilians.

Kira grabbed the handle once the chopper was on the ground, but Sam grabbed her hand, stopping her from leaving. He pulled her back around then waited until the engine noise died down.

"Don't tell me to wait here," she said knowing that was what he was about to say.

"It'll be chaos if you go in and make an announcement. We need to be discreet, gather people up quietly."

That made sense, not that she was planning on telling everyone at once that the military was about to nuke the place. But she understood that she and Sam needed to be on the same page. She gave him a nod to let him know she agreed.

Kira got out of the chopper and ran straight for the gate. There were about a dozen civilians on the other side of the fence watching her as she made way to Frances.

"Hey, Kira," he said with a grin. "Did you enjoy your vacation with Sam?"

"Frances," she replied drawing in a deep breath. "I

need you to let these people through and have them board the helicopter." She glanced back to find Sam standing outside the vessel near the open passenger door.

"Why would I do that?" he asked curiously, one dark brow arched, while the other one lowered against a muddy eye.

"We're evacuating the remaining people here to a safe location."

He pursed his lips then blew a short breath. "I'm sorry. I have my orders to keep civilians from entering the military area. Claven would tie a noose around my neck and hang me for breaking rules."

"Claven's not coming back, Frances," she said, hoping he'd hear the urgency in her voice.

"I saw that he'd left along with an armada of personnel. What's going on, Kira?"

She was utterly surprised that he didn't know. "They're nuking the base. We don't have much time to get everyone out of here. So please, just let them through."

Frances about dropped his rifle from his hands as he glanced back at the civilians standing along the fence line watching, wondering what was going on. He looked at Sam waiting near the chopper then returned his gaze to Kira.

"All right." He waved over the soldier standing near the exit gate. "Let's get these people to the chopper."

"There's only enough room for twenty people at a time," she said as she watched the soldier round up the confused people and lead them through the gate toward the chopper. "Don't spread the news or you'll create a panic. We want this to go as smoothly as possible."

Frances complied with a nod. Though she saw the fear in his eyes, he hid it bravely as she left him standing at the gate. She followed the group of men and women, helping some into the chopper until it was full. Then as Sam lifted the bird into the air, she breathed out in relief.

Their first load-up was a success. She only hoped when they got back to pick the next group up, word hadn't gotten out about what was going on. For if there was mass panic, and the people had stormed the gates to get to the hangar, they'd have no choice but to leave them there to die.

Chapter Eight

Everything went surprisingly well during the next three trips. People had heard news about the bomb and the crack in the wall on the civilian side of the base, but they still waited patiently with Frances until it was their turn to board the chopper and be flown to safety.

Another wonderful surprise was that all the men had decided the women should be saved first. So the only people left were men who were prepared to be the last ones to board, dying for the others if they had to. There was one man in his mid-forties who had grumbled that he wasn't allowed to board until the last flight, but thankfully the other men calmed him down so the flight could take off.

Now on the final approach, Kira gazed down at the final twenty-one men, including Frances and the other soldier Bernie. Her watch said they had forty-five minutes to get them boarded and out of range before the bomb dropped. She was confident they had plenty of time since it only took five minutes to get them in the chopper then another ten to fifteen to get to the airstrip in Kingfisher.

As they landed, she noticed a young woman running down the pathway toward the gate. She looked frantic. Chills spread over Kira's skin as she hopped out of the chopper and hurried toward her, hoping the east end wall hadn't collapsed.

"Help me," the woman pleaded reaching out for her. "My mother fell a little while ago and I can't wake her up."

She grasped Kira's hand then pulled her toward the one-story civilian units. "Why didn't you come earlier?" she asked, hesitating to follow her down the path.

"I was afraid to leave her side. She has heart problems and may have had a heart attack. Please come with me. I can't get her to respond."

Kira glanced back, catching Sam's attention as he stood on the pilot's side of the craft. If this woman's mother needed to be carried, she'd need a little muscle. Hopefully the men shouting at Sam to get back in the helicopter could wait a few more minutes. And not only that, but the chopper was already at its maximum capacity. Even a few more passengers could weigh it down enough they wouldn't be able to get far enough off the ground to get over the base walls.

"What's your name?" Kira asked as Sam made it to her side.

"Tina," she replied in tears. "I'm so sorry to put you through this." She glanced around Kira at the helicopter and the angry men who'd patiently waited for their turn to leave. "They don't look very happy."

"It's okay," Sam said with a nod. "Just show us where your mother is."

Tina gave a short nod as she led them quickly down the pathway between the civilian units. She didn't take notice to Sam's knowledge of her mother, though Kira did. He'd read the girl's mind to save time. Then he moved ahead, turned around and walked backward, stopping them with his palm up and out.

"Go back to the helicopter," he demanded. "Get the engine going, Kira. I'll be back there as soon as I have her mother."

"Wait," Tina pleaded. "You don't know where she is."

"It's okay," Kira said taking Tina by the hand. "He'll find her. Come on. We need to do as he says."

Tina nodded, though she had no choice as Kira pulled her back down the path. She looked terribly worried and with good reason. They were cutting it close. But this was just a minor setback. Soon they'd be in the air and making one last sweep over the hordes of undead before the place was leveled to the ground.

"What the hell's going on?" one of the men shouted in Kira's face. She maneuvered around him to help Tina up into the chopper. "Where's our pilot going?"

"Our hero is getting my mother!" Tina snapped angrily.

"Your mother's about half dead anyway," the same man spat out. Kira recognized him as Gary, the same guy that had pitched a fit over the women getting evacuated first. "That bomb's going to drop any minute. I can fly this. I say we leave them and get the hell out of here."

"Quiet!" Kira roared as she hopped up into the pilot's seat. She clenched her jaw tightly as she began the start-up procedures. "There's plenty of time left."

"How much time do we got?" Gary asked as the propeller slowly circled and the engine began to whir.

"Thirty-five minutes," she replied with a sigh. She glanced down the pathway. Still no Sam. Damn it, where was he? He should've been here by now.

Go, Kira. She heard Sam's voice in her mind. *Tina's mother is dead. The wall's been breached.*

"What?" she whispered, hands beginning to tremble. Her lips wavered as she tried to comprehend the situation. She wouldn't lift this bird off the ground until he got here. "I'm not leaving you. Just run, Sam. The helicopter's ready to take off."

I can't make it. I'm trying to keep them off long enough for you to get out of here. Go, Kira! Now!

There was a moment where all was quiet. Even the whir of the helicopter's engine had somehow silenced into a muffled hum. It was then Kira began to see the picture, of her inside that cabin, living an empty life alone in a fenced off community ... without Sam.

Fear suddenly faded as another image played in her mind-the car accident with her parents. It had happened in Rhode Island where they lived. There were so many dead overwhelming the street, some she'd even recognized as neighbors. Her dad swerved the car to miss them, but he was going too fast. The car slid off the road then head on into a tree.

The branches went through the windshield pinning her parents to the front seat, killing her dad instantly. Her mom prayed aloud that Jake would find his sister before the monsters did just before she breathed her last gurgling breath. Kira glanced over at the injured body in the seat next to her and at first couldn't tell who it was, not until he turned his bloodied face to hers.

Kira covered her mouth with her hands, eyes wet with tears. Why? Why had she seen Sam beside her? Nobody had told her he was there, and it wasn't possible. His wounds looked too severe to have survived.

She vaguely remembered crawling from the wreckage, wounded, body barely functional. One of the dead had discovered her lying on the ground, but she couldn't move fast enough to get away.

When Jake found her on the pavement outside the car, the infected man was digging into her leg. Then the next thing she knew, she'd woken up in a lab on a naval ship sailing in the middle of the Atlantic. That wasn't normal procedure for an accident victim, let alone for an infected military private with chunks of her leg missing. But nothing of this vision made any sense at all. If the accident had played out this way, then why wasn't she infected?

Kira breathed hard, shaking her head. What had happened between the accident and the naval ship? Only Jake knew the answers to that.

"I love you, Sam," she whispered, then turned back to Gary who sat staring at her, brows lowered against his muddy eyes. "You said you were a pilot. Can you fly this thing?"

"Yes," he replied, a curious expression drawn over his unshaven salt and pepper face.

"Then get up here and take over. Head Northeast to Kingfisher Airport. The coordinates are marked on the map. Can you do that?"

He nodded as she grabbed the assault rifle between the seats then opened the pilot's side door. "What about you?" he asked.

"I'm going to find Sam." She began to close the door, but stopped and leaned back in. "Find my brother Jake Spence. Tell him that I love him and that I finally remembered the accident. Tell him that I said it's okay—I'm not scared anymore."

"All right," Gary replied with another nod of his head just before Kira closed the door.

Her body trembled as she took off across the lot and down the path where Sam fought off the monsters. She didn't want to see them, couldn't fathom facing her nightmares. But she'd do anything to save him, even die for him which seemed inevitable now. The bomb would get dropped in approximately thirty minutes, hopefully before the dead caught up to them.

She reached the end of the path just in time to see one of the large units surrounded in blue light crash to the ground, blocking the small crumbling gap in the wall. The glowing light faded. She saw Sam kneeling on the ground near the entryway, a gruesome display of slain undead surrounding him in a wide circle.

"Sam!" she shouted catching his immediate attention just as the helicopter flew over her heading northeast toward the rendezvous point. It was too late to change her mind now, not that she would.

"What the hell are you doing here?" Sam shouted as he hurried up the path toward her. He caught her arms with his hands and squeezed, shaking her. "I told you to go!"

"I couldn't leave you," she replied. "I remember Sam. I remember everything … especially you!" She threw her arms around his neck and held him tightly, like a long lost soul finally finding her way home. "I've been in the dark for so many years," she whispered in his ear. "I know now that this is where I belong, here with you. I love you, Sam. I've always loved you."

Sam gently shoved her back. He no longer glared as he took her face in his hands then kissed her lips. It was a passionate kiss that swept all the bad from her mind. It didn't matter that she would die here by zombie or nuclear bomb, as long as he knew exactly how she felt.

He grabbed her hand and began to walk toward the main building. "We don't have much time left."

"Do you have a plan?"

He chuckled as he held the right side door open for her. "I always have a plan."

Sam locked the doors the moment they were inside the building. He easily pulled the iron handrail off the side entrance wall and twisted it round the metal handles, tying the two doors together.

"Just in case they make it through the barrier," he said taking Kira's hand again.

As he pulled her down the dark passageway, she wondered what his plan was. The stairwell led to the basement where they kept records. And although the downstairs was under ground and the walls enforced with thick cinderblock, it just wouldn't be deep enough to withstand a nuclear bomb. Plus, it was pitch black down there.

She shivered when they reached the stairs. Her palms were wet with sweat. She held Sam's hand tighter as he led her down into the dark.

"There should be a door near the back wall." He pulled her along through the dark. She couldn't see a thing and yet he kept the pace as if he had the place memorized. "Here it is."

"I can't see, Sam," she whispered, her teeth chattering.

"Once we're down inside I'll provide some light."

She felt his arms slide around her waist. Her feet left the ground as he held her against him tightly.

"Hold on," he said as he stepped back.

She suddenly fell downward. The trip was short as he landed on wet ground. She felt cool water on her bare legs up to her knees and shivered wishing she could see where they'd landed. By the awful scent surrounding them, she had no doubt it was the old sewer system running beneath the old airport.

A small light came on and she could finally see Sam's face. Still in his arms, he took advantage of the situation and kissed her once before setting her down on her feet. Without a word, he grabbed her hand then led her quickly down the narrow arched passageway.

Knee-deep in dark water, Kira felt awful. This was by far the most frightening thing she'd ever experienced. If she'd any idea this morning this was what she'd be doing now, she would've worn the torn pants or the coffee-stained jeans. She would've at least worn the boots and tossed the cute sandals that meant the world to her out the window.

It didn't matter what she wore now anyway. Even if they were able to evade the impact, they wouldn't get far enough to avoid the fallout.

"Here," Sam said stopping at a ladder leading upward. He handed her the small flashlight. "Stay here while I check outside."

As he quickly stepped up toward the round manhole cover, Kira shined the light down the dark passageway. Squeaks from vermin echoed around her. All she needed was to think of the nasty things crawling around at her feet. She hated rats though she didn't blame them for wanting to be down here. Maybe it was safer below the infected beings on the surface.

A deep throaty moan came from the same way they'd come. A chill crept up her spine when the tiny voices of the animals hushed to silence.

"Sam," she whispered grabbing on to the handle of the ladder. She pointed the flashlight up to find him at the top working on the manhole that seemed to be stuck. "Hurry up, Sam! There's something down here."

Her hands began to shake as again she shined the light into the dark finding a shadowed figure moving slowly toward her, sloshing in the water, moaning.

When she found the man's face with the light, he stopped his eerie moan and turned his face toward her.

His mouth was agape, blood caked on his lips and chin. The light shirt he wore was torn, filthy and stained with the same dark liquid he'd obviously feasted on. The white of his eyes seemed to glow in the light as he stood there not making a move or a sound.

It took every ounce of strength not to scream, knowing if she did it'd gather his attention again. She really didn't want to become his next meal. The thought of it made her entire body tremble.

A loud crash came from above then rolled across the surface above her. Startled, she dropped the flash light, which began to sink in the water around her ankles. In the fading light, the man began to move forward, groaning again a little more intensely than before.

That was all she could take. With him only a few feet away drawing nearer, and Sam god knows where, she opened her mouth and let out a blood curdling scream. At the moment the man lunged toward her, white light emanated from her body. It immediately streaked like a bolt of lightning, hitting the man in the chest. The force sent him flying back a good twenty feet.

Stunned, Kira inspected herself until the glow faded. A hand grasped her tightly around the wrist then pulled her up onto the ladder.

"Climb!" Sam demanded.

Finding her wits, Kira did as she was told. She

climbed quickly toward daylight, toward a familiar sound. It sounded like the generators of the base humming, but louder and less muffled. She knew then they'd made it outside the base.

When she reached the street she turned to watch Sam lift himself up out of the hole. Movement in the distance caught her attention. It was then that she found out the sound she'd heard all those years stuck behind the walls of the base wasn't from generators keeping the base functioning. It was the sound of the dead.

There were hundreds of them, some growling as they beat their fists against the crumbling outer walls of the base. Most of them were still dressed in the same clothes they'd become infected in, tattered, ripped, filthy. Others were naked, bodies deformed and decaying to a point they looked like nothing but bone and rotting flesh.

Chills spread over Kira's skin, over the chills that had been there ever since she'd let the helicopter leave without her. Frightened, she fisted the material of Sam's sleeve and wouldn't let go as he led her down the street away from the horde that thankfully seemed to have no idea they were there.

Sam opened the driver's side door of a truck. The dark blue vehicle sat on wheels so big it needed a step-ladder for the driver to get in. He waved Kira up inside and she didn't hesitate to climb in and over into the middle of the bench seat.

Sam hurried in and shut the driver's side door then turned to Kira. "This thing's been sitting here for years, so I'll need to charge the battery," he said as he pulled the lever on the bottom left side of the dash. The hood released and popped up slightly. "When you see my light, I want you to turn the key in the ignition. It might take a few tries, but we should be able to get this thing going."

She grabbed hold of his shirt before he could grasp the handle. "Don't go out there," she pleaded. "We could just make a run for it. I'm sure there's a shelter underneath one of the nearby hotels or something."

"There's not enough time to go search for shelter," Sam replied. He sighed as he palmed her face then brushed his thumb lightly across the bridge of her cheek. "I know you're scared. But I swear, I won't let anything happen to you." He kissed her lips once then leapt out of the truck.

The door slammed shut. Kira's attention went straight to the horde across the street. A few of them on the edge of the group turned their way. Her stomach twisted into knots as Sam's light began to show through the thin strip between the raised hood and truck. That was her cue.

With a shaky hand, she turned the ignition. Nothing happened. She immediately tried again, but still there was no coughing or sputtering, not even a horrible clicking noise came from the engine of this beast.

"Hang on!" Sam hopped up onto the front of the truck.

While he struggled with something, jerking a hose or a connector back and forth, Kira looked at the wandering dead. A few more of them had turned their way, slowly discovering there were living beings here, flesh they were eager to consume.

"Try again," Sam said as he slid to the ground.

She turned the ignition. The engine coughed but didn't start. A thunderous boom came from the exhaust startling her as Sam slammed the hood down. He hurried back around and hopped into the truck just as the dead began shuffling their way.

"Hurry up Sam," Kira said as he turned the key. The truck finally coughed, sputtered, then started. There was another loud backfire then the engine growled to full life.

When he shifted the truck into first gear, one of the bodies hopped up onto the truck. It was a woman, naked, decayed as she crawled across the hood, eyes on Kira who leaned further back in the seat.

"Put on your seatbelt!" he demanded as he stepped his foot down, forcing the truck to lurch forward.

She looked down to find the middle belt stuffed down in the seat. As much as she dreaded moving away from Sam, she slid to the passenger side and belted herself in with the shoulder strap.

Sam sped up, weaving the truck back and forth around wrecked cars and trucks. The desiccated body slid across the dusty hood desperate to hold on as it attempted to crawl up to the windshield. Its eyes were still locked on Kira.

"Damn it, get off!" Sam shouted as he pulled the truck close to the guard rail on Kira's side. The sound of metal scraping against metal hurt Kira's ears. Her body broke out in chills as she held her palms over her ears to block out the sound until the guard rail finally turned into a cement wall.

The force of the truck hitting the wall sent the body sliding off to the side. Sam turned the truck into it again hoping the blow would knock the body off, but it held on tightly. It grabbed hold of the side view mirror and pulled itself up. It opened its mouth showing rotting teeth and bone as it screeched, sending a different kind of chill down Kira's spine. Then, without warning, the thing punched its bony fist through the windshield.

Sam swerved. The truck hit the cement wall head first then immediately stalled out. Tears sprung to Kira's eyes, but not out of fear alone. There was something else, something she'd never felt before. It was warm as it dripped from her brow.

She touched her temple with her fingers then brought her hand forward. Blood. Strange she'd been injured in the crash, but she couldn't feel any pain.

"Kira," Sam whispered. Her eyes locked with his. He looked terribly worried and yet, he gave a sort of half-grin, the kind that let her know everything was going to be all right.

A light caught Kira's eyes and she followed it. "What's happening to me?" she asked recognizing it as the same glow that came from her in the sewer, the one that knocked the dead away. This was the same light that reminded her of Sam's.

He turned the key. The engine sputtered and steam rose from the fractured hood. He turned the key again then the engine finally roared to life.

As he pulled out on the road, Kira glanced down at the body that was crushed in the accident. It's top half had been severed completely. The creature crawled toward them with its hands, dragging its bottom half behind it.

Kira felt ill now. With the light she'd somehow conjured around her now gone, she felt pain from the wound on her head, and her neck and shoulders were sore.

Now on the road out of here, she pulled her seatbelt off and slid close to Sam. She moved her arm beneath his then grasped his hand hoping they'd make it to the safe boundary before the military dropped the bomb. But they only had fifteen minutes left. And though they'd be out of range for the initial impact, the radioactive fallout would most assuredly catch up to them.

Chapter Nine

Kira checked Claven's watch still latched loosely around her wrist. She was surprised it'd held on for the past day of chaos. But now, it didn't matter if the watch still hung on or not. It didn't matter how far out of the city they'd traveled. It just wouldn't be enough.

"We're not going to make it Sam," Kira said as she leaned her aching head against his shoulder. She gazed at the speedometer. One hundred twenty miles per hour. The gas light was on. It'd only be a matter of time before they ran out of fuel completely.

"Don't give up, Kira," Sam replied, keeping his gaze on the desolate road ahead of them. His lips were pursed as if he was angry and yet she saw sorrow in his eyes. He knew there wasn't enough time.

"Tell me what happened after you found me," she said catching his eyes briefly before he turned back to the road. "I was infected, Sam. Why didn't I become one of ... them?"

He didn't say anything at first. But when she nudged his ribs gently with her elbow, he gave a short nod.

"About eleven years ago, there were twenty willing subjects, soldiers who underwent a series of injections called Series-6, or S6. The serum was supposed to open up inactive parts of the brain. It was a success for some of us. Others weren't so lucky."

"So that's how you became a super soldier," she stated, though that only confirmed what she'd already suspected.

His grin widened. "I was twenty-three with the strength of a hundred men. I was invincible ... and dangerous. It took a few years of training to get my powers under control, but I managed to do it. We all managed."

"What happened to the others?"

His lips stooped into a frown. "Their bodies mutated and eventually died, at least that's what the scientists believed until one of the bodies went missing. Some civilians found him on the street outside the facility. When they took him to the hospital he turned violent and began killing everyone. It was a massacre."

"Oh," she gasped, chills spreading over her skin. "So that's how this all began. The virus was in the serum. I was injected, too," she whispered.

"Jake was pretty upset about the accident. He'd just lost his parents and didn't want to lose you too. When he found you lying on the ground with that thing digging into your leg, he took you to the lab and forced the injections."

She shivered. "What if it hadn't worked?"

"He was willing to take the chance." He brought

her hand to his lips. "And I didn't want to go on without you."

She raised her free hand to his unshaven face. "We're together now," she said as she lifted her dress to her hips then straddled his lap. "That's all that matters."

At the moment she released him from the confines of his slacks, the truck's engine sputtered. It coughed a few more times then finally stalled out.

"How much time do we have left?" Sam asked as the truck quickly slowed in silence.

Kira glanced at the watch, eyes blurring with tears as she slid down the length of his shaft, taking him deep inside her. "Eight minutes," she breathed out then kissed his lips as he thrust upward. "This is the way to die, Sam, in your arms, making love to you," she moaned, holding him tight around his neck.

"I don't want you to die." He massaged her hips, guiding her up then pulling her quickly down. "You're too beautiful," he whispered.

When the truck finally stopped near the edge of the road, Kira sighed. Eight minutes until impact, then another five or so until the fallout reached their zone.

She leaned back against the steering wheel then closed her eyes, seeing again the vision of Sam's home in Hawaii. The blue ocean roared in the distance as its waves rolled onto the beach. If only they were there now making love like this beneath the palm trees, not in this old truck.

"This is my fault, Sam," she said opening her eyes. "If I'd just stayed at the retreat, we wouldn't be in this situation now."

"You couldn't have known." He flashed a half-grin, thrusting again. "You saved a lot of lives today, Kira. That's something to be proud of. You're a hero to all of those people who would've died if you hadn't come. They'll remember you."

She moved forward against him. Face to face with him now, she gazed into those blue gems. Then she pressed her lips against his.

He tightened his hold on her hips, thrusting urgently as she pressed her thighs tightly against him. "I love you, Sam," she whispered then pushed her tongue in his mouth, licking, wanting more of him.

His hand went to the back of her head, pulling her as close as she could go until they came together. Then suddenly, there was a bright flash. As Kira breathed hard into his shoulder, eyes shut tight, she whispered what she believed would be her final words. "I have always loved you, Sam."

A strange calm took over the fear. Everything happening seemed so surreal, as if they were protected from all the bad outside. It was as if this very place, him still inside her, had some sort of healing effect, a barrier that would protect them from harm.

"Look," Sam said, gently moving her off his lap. He buttoned his slacks then leaned forward against the steering wheel.

She followed his gaze pointed at the darkening sky. There was a light shining over the small mountain on the horizon. It looked like a star at first. But the more she watched it, the closer it came.

Sam quickly jumped out of the truck. He motioned

for her to come with him and she complied, following him out onto the road. As the light grew in size, so did the whir of an engine.

"It's Jake!" Sam called out as he waved his arms flagging him down.

As excited as Kira was to see the chopper turn their way, she felt sure there still wasn't enough time to make it to the safe zone. But as the chopper landed just before them, hope washed over her.

"Come on!" Jake shouted from the helicopter's door. He caught her hand and pulled her in followed by Sam.

Kira saw Sam's worried gaze knowing he thought the same thing. Even at top speed, there was no way they'd be able to outrun this. It might take a day or two for the radiation sickness to kick in, but they were going to die regardless. And now, because of Jake's refusal to leave her behind, he'd die as well.

"It'll be okay, Kira," Jake shouted over the helicopter's loud whir. "The wind has shifted to the south. We're in the safe zone."

"We are?" she asked a rush of excitement coursing through her.

Jake gave her a nod. "We're going to be fine."

Kira sighed in relief. She smiled as she looked at Sam. Though he flashed a half grin, that worried look he had a few minutes ago still lingered.

"Is something wrong?" she asked him. He glanced at Jake then returned his gaze to hers. That said it all. Something was obviously going on between the two men. Maybe they were having a conversation, one she couldn't hear, at least, not at first. Then the whispers came.

Are you sure she's ready? Jake's voice entered her mind as the chopper's hum faded.

With proper care, came another man's reply, though his voice was very distant. It sounded like Sam, but she just wasn't sure. *Let's not force the issue, in case it doesn't work.*

It's a little late for that. She made the decision when she left the car.

I didn't force her to get out of the car, if that's what you're insinuating. She made up her own mind, just as I thought she'd do.

After you put the memories in her head, Jake insisted.

It was time for her to discover her past, the other man demanded, still a bit fuzzy though it was sounding more and more like Sam.

You mean it was time she remembered her past with you. There was silence for a few seconds and Kira wondered if she'd lost the link, but then Jake spoke again. *It doesn't matter anymore. She's still one of us. Maybe this time, she'll recover from this fully.*

What happened to you Jake? You've protected her all these years from being discovered. Now suddenly you want to use her.

The world's a lot safer now, Jake replied. *It won't be long until the threat is completely eradicated. She will be like us again, I'll make sure of it. But she'll be weak. She'll need to learn to protect herself in case she runs into strays.*

They won't let her out in society. Once they find out about her, they'll do the same thing to her what they have planned for us.

Jake lowered his brows. "They won't do anything to us."

"Seriously Jake? You know as well as I do that it won't be long until we're decommissioned."

"Decommissioned?" Kira said aloud, catching the men's immediate attention. Like flying out of a dream, the helicopter's whir became loud in her ears, and the voices she'd heard before dissipated. "I didn't mean to eavesdrop on your conversation," she continued, ignoring their surprised reactions. "But why would they want to decommission the only people who can fight these … things?"

"We've been doing this for years, Kira," Sam replied, his stunned glance turned into an easy grin. "The threat is pretty low now that they've destroyed the last infested base."

"It just takes one to get it going again," she remarked.

Sam nodded. "You don't have to remind me. But the people in charge don't see it that way. They think they're safe inside their new settlement."

"So why can't they keep you guys around just in case? It doesn't make sense."

Sam gave a short sigh then grasped her hand in his. "We're carriers of the virus. It may have affected us differently, but the threat is still inside us."

That made sense. Now she understood why Jake had protected her all these years. She should be angry with him. After all, he'd put the lives of everyone on the base in danger letting her stay without knowledge of what she carried in her bloodstream, if that was what he was saying. The conversation was a bit confusing.

"So what do you mean by decommissioned? Are they planning on killing us?"

She watched Sam and Jake share another glance before Sam replied. "No, Kira. They'll make us leave the settlement." He threw one more quick glance at Jake, then Kira knew he wasn't telling the truth.

"You'll tell the military about me," she demanded. "If I'm a threat to them, then I won't do anything to jeopardize everything those people have worked for. You should've told me from the beginning instead of protecting me!"

She let go of Sam's hand and clenched her fists tightly. How could they have kept such a terrible thing from her, putting civilian lives at risk. It would've been easier to know the truth. She could've been trained to be strong rather than live her life sheltered and scared behind thick walls.

The moment the helicopter set down on the ground, she was out, walking across the paved lot toward the warehouse. She ignored Sam's voice calling for her as she went into the building to find all the civilians she'd saved that day. They immediately broke out in applause.

Kira's face warmed as she stood near the open hangar door. She had a mind to turn and run, not wanting such an unworthy greeting. If they only knew what was inside her, they'd have shunned her instead. They'd want to kill her.

With that thought, she turned. Tears sprung to her eyes as she leaned against the steel wall outside, hiding as the applause quickly ended.

She heard their voices in her mind, many of them echoing, whispering, shouting, why was this happening, or what was going on. This gift was more like a curse. She wished to God the infection had gone into someone else or at least never was revealed.

Sam stepped out of the warehouse. He came to her side then leaned back against the wall as he looked at her.

"Are you okay?"

"No," she replied. "I hear everything. Their thoughts, their fears ... how do I shut the voices off?"

"Think about something else."

She leaned her head back against the building and closed her eyes. The image of the beach, Sam's home in Hawaii, entered her mind. He was with her, beside her, holding her hand. Then his mouth was against hers, tongue on tongue. When he pulled away, the voices silenced, leaving nothing but the sound of the ocean roaring in the distance.

"I love you Kira," Sam said, his sandy hair moving in the breeze. His eyes sparkled like diamonds in sunlight, so surreal. "Go now. The helicopter's empty. The engine's warm. Come here and make a life for yourself. With me. I'm here, Kira. I'll take care of you. All you have to do is open your eyes."

Kira opened her eyes to find Sam standing before her gazing down at her. Even in twilight, those gems of his glittered beautifully. His hair moved in the gentle breeze, just as it had done in the vision, and she took that as a sign.

Sam immediately grasped her hand and led her to

the helicopter. As Kira hopped up into the passenger side, Sam fired the engine. In no time, they were in the air heading west over the flat of land.

"There's only enough gas for a few hours travel before you need to set down and search for more," Sam said through the headset.

Kira nodded, then caught a chill. In her excitement of Sam whisking her away into the sunset, she hadn't thought of running out of gas on the way. She dreaded stepping foot on the ground, especially in the dark.

But as frightening as it was, she knew Sam would get her safely to her destination. Being with him made her fear manageable as she kept in the front of her mind the vision of him on the beach. It didn't matter how long it took or how difficult it'd be to get there, she would see it through. She would survive.

Chapter Ten

Kira sneezed from all the dust that'd settled in the air from the cleaning she'd done that morning. She'd opened the windows on each side of the house to air it out, but there wasn't enough breeze today to blow the dust through, not like yesterday's wind anyway.

They'd only been in Hawaii three days. The first day was spent scoping the house and its surroundings, to make sure there weren't any dead people walking around. That night and the better part of the next day was spent catching up on sleep they'd missed in the time it'd taken to get here, though the days seemed like a blink of an eye, so easy of a transition that the trip didn't seem like it had happened at all. Then that evening, they rummaged through the well-stocked pantry on the lower part of the house.

Sam's father had kept an excellent supply of emergency rations: water, canned foods, batteries, and just about everything else they needed for survival purposes. There was also a generator that Sam decided should only be used in real emergencies or when he had a chance to thoroughly scour the grounds outside. If there were walking dead close by, the noise of the generator would attract them. They weren't ready for confrontation yet.

Kira thought it was sad that his family hadn't survived long enough to use all these good things especially now that the canned goods were well past the expiration date. Lucky for them, Sam's mother had planted a garden in the back of the house that was now overgrown and loaded with fruits and vegetables. Some of the vines had even grown over the house to offer a little extra security, or at least, make Kira feel less exposed to the outside world. Even though she hadn't seen any walking dead since they'd left the base, she knew they were out there somewhere just waiting to find them.

Sam was outside repairing a few damaged tiles on the roof of the house. One of the bedroom windows on the coast side had been damaged, most likely due to one of the many storms that had hit the coast. Other than that and the mounds of dust that had gathered on all the furniture, the house was in pretty good shape.

Kira was hesitant to step outside, but she drew in a deep breath, grabbed up the giant bowl she'd found in the bottom cabinet in the kitchen, then left the safety of the house for the backyard. It wasn't really a yard, but more jungle-like as she walked around vines and trees to pick fruits and vegetables. She actually began to enjoy the walk, loving the way the soft grass felt beneath her bare feet. The thin yellow sundress she'd found in the bedroom closet tickled her skin so softly that it felt like feathers brushing against her. She couldn't remember ever feeling anything quite like it.

She turned back and found Sam kneeling on the roof. His bare chest glistened in the sunlight as he stapled a new tile down. He was so sexy.

Kira breathed deeply. Caught up on sleep, belly full from breakfast, she felt relaxed. There was nothing to be afraid of here. She had everything she could ever want. This was their place now, and she'd be damned if anyone or anything would take it from them.

Kira shivered as a light gust of wind lifted her hair just enough for a few strands to move against her face. She turned to find the sky darkening slightly, the sun disappearing behind dark clouds.

"A storm's coming," Sam called out to her. "Let's go in."

Kira nodded. She grabbed a pineapple from the large bush beside her and went straight into the house. She set the bowl down on the clean table then hurried to the large window on the wall in front.

As it began to rain, Sam quickly stepped down the ladder to the ground. He made his way through the front door just as the rain turned to a downpour.

"Got the roof finished just in time," he said with a snicker. He ran his hand through his wet hair then flashed a remarkable grin.

There was something different about him, something Kira couldn't quite put her finger on. He looked happy. But for some reason it seemed forced.

"Is something wrong?" Kira asked as she leaned

against his wet body. She gazed into his eyes. Strange how those gems weren't as blue as they normally were. It was as if she stared into someone else's eyes, not the Sam she was desperately in love with.

"Nothing's wrong," he replied pulling away from her. "I'm just soaked. Let me go dry off and change."

He left her standing near the front door staring out at the ocean. She shivered as a strange feeling washed over her. It was as if she stood in an empty room. The scenic view was just a ruse, a mere image on the wall that was meant to look real.

A chill crept over her body. She felt weak, cold.

She locked the front door and went back to the kitchen. The dark blue candle she'd lit the night before was still sitting on the counter. It'd flickered throughout most of the night, and yet it looked fairly new.

"Sam," she called out as she inspected the black wick. When he didn't answer, she went down the hall to investigate. "Sam, where are you?"

"I'm here, Kira," he said appearing in the doorway of the bedroom. "Don't you remember?" His hair was dry. His body was clothed in jeans and a white T-shirt. He leaned to the side against the frame casting the same glowing grin he'd flashed just moments before. "Are you all right? You look like you've just seen a ghost."

"I don't know," she replied in earnest. Something was definitely off here.

She ran her fingers through his dry hair. Strange— it was wet just a few moments ago. He'd changed his clothes so quickly too. When his eyes slightly faded into a much duller color, she took a step back.

"What's going on Sam?" she asked, swallowing the lump in her throat. That nice feeling she'd had in the garden quickly turned to fear she'd never felt before.

Sam slumped. His breath turned ragged as he fell to his knees before her. He opened up his arms and looked down as a giant gash spread across his chest. Blood stained his shirt as he now lay in the back seat of a car.

"No!" Kira cried, reaching out to touch him. "Don't leave me!"

The image of the house, their beautiful abode they'd planned to spend their lives in suddenly turned into a darkened room. Then her beloved Sam, as he lifted his eyes to hers, faded from her sight.

Kira suddenly opened her eyes. She lay on a small cot staring up at a dark gray ceiling. The walls around her were the same color, steel like the barrier in the ship she'd woken up in six years ago. The room creaked with an eerie song that sent chills up her spine.

It took her a few weak tries, but she managed to slowly sit up and look down the length of the cot. She'd been dressed in a white gown. The sleeves were long and covering the goose bumps spreading quickly over her chilled skin. Ignoring the ache in her head, she moved her tired legs over the edge of the bed.

"Sam," she whispered, then coughed. She pressed her dry cracked lips together and breathed quickly through her nose, trying to catch her breath. "Sam!"

she tried again, still in a whisper.

When nobody answered, she rose from the bed and stepped slowly on wobbly legs toward the only door in the room. The oval shaped door creaked loudly when she opened it. She cringed and hoped wherever she was they were friendly and not the dead wandering waiting to eat her flesh. She stepped out into an empty hall, so narrow that she knew she wasn't on a ship.

She heard voices up ahead. Sliding her hands along the steel wall of the hall to keep her balance, she hurried toward them in hopes to find out what was going on. Where was Sam? Where was the beautiful place she'd just come from?

The moment she stepped into the light of the room, she saw two familiar faces—Jake and Kyle. They looked peaked, pale and weaker than before as they stood at a lit up console with two other men she didn't recognize. When they saw her, they all took a step back, eyes widened, almost as if her presence frightened them.

"Jake?" she whispered as she inched slowly toward him, reaching out to take hold. "Jake, what's happened?"

"Get the doctor!" Jake ordered one of the men who immediately took off down the short hall on the right side of the room.

He backed away from her as she moved closer. Seeing her brother afraid, she stopped next to the controls and glanced around. It was just as she thought. She was in the belly of a submarine.

"Kira?" Jake whispered in awe. He started to move

toward her but was stopped when Kyle placed his big hand on his chest.

"Jake," she said turning her gaze on him. "I was in a house a few moments ago with Sam. How did I get here?"

"Sam?" Jake sounded rather surprised. "That's not possible, Kira. You must have been … dreaming?" He curled his finger against his lips in thought. "I have noticed an increase in REM lately."

"Where's Sam?" she asked wondering why he'd said it wasn't possible.

"Don't you remember?" He lowered his hand to his side and arched his brows. "Sam's dead, Kira. He has been for six years now, ever since the accident with our parents."

"No!" Kira cried out. She covered her face with her hands and cried. "You're lying," she continued angrily, wanting to hurt him for saying such a terrible thing. "I was just with him. Why would you lie to me?" she shrieked.

"He died, Kira, with our parents. I'm … sorry."

Kira shook her head. "It's not true." She took another step toward him. When he quickly backed away, she stopped again. "Why are you afraid of me?"

Jake sighed. He gave Kyle and the other man a nod, sending them out of the room before he turned his attention back on her. His face looked a little grim, but it gave her a strange sense of ease.

"You've been in a coma for six years, ever since the accident."

She gasped, trying to make sense of this. Surely she couldn't have dreamed everything that had happened. No, this was definitely the dream. This was a nightmare she needed to wake from.

"I was with Sam. We were in Hawaii at his parents' house. Wake me up!" she cried grasping her head with her hands. "Please! Wake me up!"

"Calm down, honey," Jake said. He hesitantly took hold of her wrists and pulled them down to her sides. When she looked at him, he immediately let her go and stepped back once more. "Kira, honey, you need to remember what happened. You're awake now," he insisted, a dumbfounded expression on his face.

"I—I can't remember," she stammered, confused, heartbroken. "Please explain to me why I feel this way. Why am I so cold? I need to know why I was with Sam?"

"Possibly what you've dreamed are preserved memories of your time with him."

"Preserved memories?"

"Well ..." Jake shrugged then scratched the top of his head. "Right before the outbreak you and Sam got married. You spent your honeymoon together at his family retreat in Hawaii. The virus broke out when you returned home. While Sam was trying to get you and our parents to safety, the tire on the car blew out. Everyone died but you."

Kira hunched over, feeling ill. "But you and Sam took me to the navy ship in the Atlantic," she said, her voice again in a whisper. "You forced them to inject me with the S6."

"How'd you know about S6?" he asked, his face pale in surprise. "There's no way you could know about the serum."

"Sam told me about it. That's how you got your powers. That's how the virus began."

Jake chuckled. It wasn't a nervous laugh, but one laced with puzzlement. "Kira. The S6 serum is an experimental drug, an antidote we've been trying to develop for the past five years. We've been working on it since the virus spread." He threw her a nervous glance. "You ... you were infected. And now ... " He studied her face, moving closer to her. "May I?" he asked then turned her around before she could respond.

He lifted the bottom of her gown up just enough to look at the scar on the back of her leg. She followed his path, finding nothing but fair skin and a faint red mark where the unsightly scar used to be.

"The wound has healed," Jake whispered. He massaged his fingers through her hair inspecting her scalp. "The empty follicles are filling in!" he announced excitedly.

"Empty follicles?" she thought. Though it was difficult to concentrate on anything else besides the fact that Sam was dead, and had been for a long time, she ogled. What in the world did she look like?

"This is amazing!" he said as one of the men who had left earlier came into the room with another man dressed in a white lab coat. "Look at this, Dr. Claven. Her wound is clearing. That last injection must have taken a few weeks to take effect. But it's obviously working!"

"Take me to a mirror," Kira demanded feeling like a rat in a science experiment, and that wasn't far from the truth as she saw it now.

Kyle glanced at Dr. Claven then looked at her. "I'm not sure you're ready for that yet, Kira."

"Just let me see!" she shouted angrily. She wiped tears from her face, scratching her skin with rigid dry fingers.

As Jake led her down the hall, she gazed at her hands. They were extremely dry and thin, pale as if lacking in blood flow. She drew in a deep breath then held it for a long moment as he led her into a small room with a tiny cot and a full length mirror on the wall beside it. She hesitated for a moment beside the bed, wondering if she really wanted to see.

If her skin resembled her hands, she'd look like death, like the monsters from her nightmare. If she had been one of the dead, though kept alive for five years by experimentation, this would be difficult to swallow. Fearful and a little hesitant, she made her way to the mirror on the wall.

When she first saw the thing in the mirror she turned away. Scared of facing the truth, that she was one of them, she looked at Jake who leaned against the short arched doorframe. He didn't need to say anything. She could see the hurt, the sorrow and anger in his bright blue eyes. It pained him to see his little sister in turmoil, waking to find the gruesome face staring back at her was indeed hers.

Kira forced herself to turn back around. Lifeless eyes looked into the mirror. They weren't blue anymore, but pale and wet with tears. Her cheeks were sunken in, blackened around her ghastly eyes. And she could tell the frame beneath her long white gown was thin and frail.

She fell to her knees and sobbed in her hands. Her throat clenched but all that came out was a haunting hiss, one she'd heard before. It was the same awful sound the woman on the hood of the truck had made. In fact, her face was just like hers.

"Don't worry about your appearance, Kira," Jake said in a solemn voice as he gently picked her up off the floor until she stood before him. He didn't seem scared anymore as he pulled her into his arms and held her close to his chest, stroking the back of her head. "Your heart is still beating, as do all the people suffering in the world. The virus opened up a part of the brain that humans obviously can't handle."

"Why did you save me?" she cried softly.

"I couldn't bear to let you wander the world alone. I brought you here while we searched for the cure. I'm so sorry it took so long," he whispered in her ear. "But you're here now." He leaned her back and his mouth curved upward. "You'll be okay."

Kira nodded as she gazed into her brother's sincere eyes. "Are there any others?" she asked.

"No. You're the only one who has shown improvement so far."

A young man entered the room, out of breath and wildly beaming. He leaned his palms on his knees then pointed with his finger toward the door.

"Sir!" he said, trying to catch his breath. "They're coming out of it, sir! Just like her, they're all waking up and asking what's going on!"

Jake let go of Kira and backed away. "I'll be right back!" he exclaimed excitedly then quickly left the room.

Kira turned her attention on the reflection in the mirror. The image wasn't a lie. All this time she had indeed been dreaming. Jake had kept her going, but for what reason?

She understood he needed subjects to test the formulas on. She understood Jake's reason to obsess, knowing he went through a lot of pain to find the cure to bring her back to the living. But without Sam here? She didn't want to live without him. There was no point in being alive when the love of her life was dead.

She sat down on the floor and brought her knees to her chest. It was too difficult to believe. He'd been so close to her in her mind. Five years she'd slept, living to be with him, loving him since she could remember. So how could this be reality when it felt so horribly wrong?

Chapter Eleven

According to Jake, the distress call came in about 4 a.m. pacific time. He'd woken Kira up a few minutes after, which excited her. The last call they'd received had given them a reason to pop up to the surface to have a look around. Even though it ended up being an old recording, one sent out to see if anyone else was alive, it was nice to see the sun shining for a change. And though today would be an excellent day to find other people who had survived the virus, it'd be a wonderful thing to draw a breath of fresh air into her lungs.

It'd been three months since she'd woken up from her five-year sleep. She was still a bit thin and pale. But that was changing due to the plentiful stock of food packets in the submarine's tiny mess hall, and the continued tests Jake kept running on her.

The pigment of her eyes had turned a deep shade of blue. Though they were a little darker than she remembered them to be, it was so much better than the frightening, pallid color from before.

She was almost back to her physical self, the self she remembered while in her coma. Her dark hair was short due to the new hair growing in, but at least she hadn't gone completely bald. She'd actually found a little solace here among the other cured people who'd confessed they'd also dreamed during their sleep. But none of the dreams had been quite as vivid as hers.

Her heart was still mending over the loss of Sam. She missed him so much she cried for him every night. She'd dream of him smiling that gorgeous smile as he held her in his arms looking out on the ocean blue. She remembered they'd eloped when she was only eighteen. It was also clear now that they'd spent their honeymoon at his parents getaway in Hawaii, the same house they'd planned to spend the rest of their lives in.

They'd spent two weeks on that sandy shore in seclusion, making love beneath the palm trees. They'd wanted to begin a family as soon as they returned home to Rhode Island, but never had the chance.

Sam was a soldier in the military, a special operative just like Jake was, though Jake was more scientist than combatant. They'd even enlisted together as teens followed by Kira who'd found her place in administration. After the virus broke out, they were all sent to their units, where Jake went first. But Sam and Kira never had a chance to go.

Funny how clear everything was now. With no gaps in her memory, she knew this imperfect life was indeed the real one. Whatever the outcome, she was willing to accept it and move on. And the only place she could think of to spend the remainder of her life was in that house along the beach in Hawaii, the house that was a wedding present from Sam's family.

Now only an hour away from her destination, the call came in. It wasn't so much a distress call, but was the detection of a radio beacon located just off the Hawaiian coast. The beacon came from what looked like an old weather buoy floating in the water near the reef. Someone had attached a radio device to it in hopes to attract the living to their location.

"We're almost on it now," Jake said with a nod to the few men sitting at the controls. "Go full stop and let's surface."

Kira couldn't wait to have a look around top side. She held on to the edge of the seat as the submarine veered back. The sonar beeped, increasing in speed as they ventured toward the surface of the water, until finally the vessel emerged.

"Let's go take a look," Jake said when the ship calmed.

Kira followed him down the hall. One of the men had already unsealed the hatch near the end of the corridor and light was shining down. The breeze blew warm into the room and the breathtaking scent of the sea filled her senses.

She followed Jake up the ladder to the deck. It took her eyes only a moment to adjust to the sunlight, then she saw the calm blue ocean lapping around the sides of the vessel. In the distance was land—the Hawaiian coast, a beauty she called home. Ever since she'd woken, she'd dreamed of this place.

It had called to her like a siren song. Though this was the place she desperately wanted to be, she wasn't so sure she wanted to stay here alone.

Jake wasn't convinced that he wanted to stay, finding the undersea life fit for him. But she was determined to at least get him to land long enough to scope the place out and make sure it was safe. She told him that he couldn't stay on the submarine for the rest of his life, that five years was long enough to hide from his destiny which was to cure the world. It was a good argument for her, one that made him think seriously about coming with her.

"We'll detach and take the boats to the shore," Jake said to everyone standing on the deck. There were twenty people now. Including Kira, five were survivors of the virus.

Kira could see how scared they were. She too felt the same way. But if they were to make any kind of life for themselves, then this island would be the opportune place. It was secluded and had everything they needed to survive. If there were any ill people left wandering the island, the scientists on this vessel could give them the antidote. And if there was anyone living here, she was sure they'd be happy to see them arrive.

Jake took Kira by the hand and led her to the bright orange raft. After the others were safely inside, they took off toward land.

As the boat skipped across the waves, Jake scanned the beach in the distance with wary eyes. Kira's gaze followed but found nothing moving across the white sand. However, she did plant her eyes on the familiar large-windowed house set against lush green vines scaling upward from the backyard.

Her heart sank believing Sam should be here. This was their home. Tears welled in her eyes, but she quickly wiped them away when they landed on the shore.

The moment her feet hit the warm sand, she set out toward the house. Jake called out for her to wait, but she wouldn't listen. She didn't want to listen. All she wanted to do was go home and live her life in solitude. Even if the virus caught up to her and she died again, it wouldn't matter. She'd join Sam in the next life.

She hurried up the sandy path to the front door. It was unlocked, so she didn't hesitate to go inside. Hit with the feeling she was home, she sighed as she glanced around at the familiar surroundings.

The place was clean just as it was that day she'd spent in her dream, just before waking from the coma. On the kitchen counter sat a bowl with a pineapple. It was a strange sensation, one that made her walk to it. She picked the heavy fruit up in her hands and held it out, inspecting it. It'd been freshly picked. That meant someone had taken residence in this house.

As excited as this made her, she reminded herself Sam was dead. There was no way this freshly picked fruit was his doing. She set it back down on the table and gazed at it with tears in her eyes. "If only," she thought solemnly.

"Don't ... move," she heard a man's voice come from behind her. The cock of a gun sent chills up her spine. "Who are you? And what are you doing in my house?"

"Your house?" she replied, a little shaken that this stranger had taken refuge here. "You're the one that's trespassing."

A moment of silence went by. It deafened her, and she hoped this man wouldn't take her comment as aggression. She turned slightly, wanting to see him, to plead with him that this place was her destiny, not his. He didn't stop her from turning around.

The man was a little scruffy. He looked tired, but oddly familiar underneath long blond hair and a short beard. His blue eyes stood out in the sunlit room, and it was then she realized who he was.

"Frank?" she whispered. How could she have forgotten about Sam's older brother?

He lowered the gun and inspected her closely. "Kira?" he said then took a step toward her. He scooped her up into his arms as she wrapped her arms around his neck and held tightly. "Oh my God, Kira, you're alive!"

"I am," she replied, laughing. She was so happy, ecstatic to find Frank here. He reminded her so much of Sam that it almost felt like she was in his arms … almost.

"This doesn't make sense," Frank said gently pulling back, grasping her face between his palms. "Last I heard you'd been infected. Everyone told us you were dead!"

"I'm all right though," she said excitedly. "It's true I was infected, but Jake found the cure. There isn't a trace left in my bloodstream."

"Jake?" he said with a robust laugh. His eyes widened. "Jake is here, too?"

"He's here too, Frank … on the beach. There are other survivors with him as well."

Frank quickly strode to the front window. "Well, I'll be damned! There's the big jerk now." He snickered then turned back to Kira. "Stay here. Make yourself at home. I'm going to greet my old friend." He hurried to her then kissed her cheek with a loud smack. "You just don't know how great it is to see you," he said as he backed toward the front door. "This is such a wondrous day."

From the window Kira watched him run down the path to the beach. When he gave Jake a big bear hug, swinging him in all directions, it made her laugh … but cry all the more. It was selfish to think the virus had taken the wrong brother. Not that she wasn't happy to see Frank alive and well, but she desperately wished it were Sam instead.

She bowed her head, then leaned her temple against the window. At that moment, she heard the front door on the house creak open. She turned to find another man come in and shut the door. And when he spoke, her heart immediately skipped.

"I'm back Frank," came his familiar tone, a little more gruff than it used to be. He closed the door behind him then gave a long sigh. "I thought you were going to fix the tile on the roof. The next rain's going to put a hole in the ceiling."

He turned toward the room then immediately stopped, eyes planted right on her. It took a moment to register that he was here, alive and well, when all this time he'd been dead. And maybe it was just as strange for him seeing a ghost from the past, one who had been dead for over five years.

"Sam," she whispered.

"This is a joke, right?" he said angrily, jaw clenching and unclenching. "You're dead. Damn it," he breathed out then closed his eyes tightly. He shook his head as if trying to remove the image of her from his mind. "I'm dreaming again. Damn, these visions won't stop!"

"No, Sam." She stepped again toward him desperate to touch his shadowed jaw. "I'm here. I'm alive."

He opened his eyes. Though leery, he stood his ground until she was standing before him. She reached up and hesitantly slid her palm across his peaked face. His chest suddenly rose and fell, breath rampant as if he'd just run miles. He fell to his knees, pulling her down to the floor with him.

"You're real." He placed his hand over hers, putting pressure against his cheek as he massaged her skin. "How is this possible?"

"Jake saved me."

Sam's lips spread into a grin. "Jake!" he said with a laugh, then tears immediately welled in his eyes. He leaned his head against her chest and slowly shook his head. "I'm so sorry, Kira. I'm so ... so sorry."

"Why are you sorry?" she asked, unable to hold back her tears. She took his face in her hands and pulled his head up so she could look into his eyes.

"I searched for your body when I woke up, but you were gone. I had no idea ... "

She slid her arms around his neck and leaned her temple against his. "I thought I'd lost you forever. If I'd known you were still alive—damn it!" he shouted, startling her. "I should've known!"

"We're together now," she whispered, then pressed her lips against his. "That's all that matters now."

He slid his arms around her waist and pulled her against him as he stood on his feet. He lifted her up off the floor and slowly twirled her around, his mouth never parting from hers. She knew now that everything would be all right. Everything felt completely right. Whether in reality or dream, fate had seen to it they were forever united. And if this reality just happened to be another wonderful dream, she hoped she'd never wake up.

◆ ◆ ◆

Angela Steed

Born in Seattle, Washington, the author grew up in a small town on the Oregon Coast. After living in Portland, Oregon, she moved to the beautiful Appalachian Mountains of West Virginia where she lives with her husband and two daughters. In addition to being a novelist, Angela is a licensed realtor, freelance writer and computer specialist.

www.AngelaSteed.com